"I didn't reenlist. I'm living in Jeffersville now."

Clay hadn't seen that coming.

"You shouldn't have done it for me," he said.

She stiffened and took a step back. "I did it for *me*."

"I'm sorry. I didn't mean to make assumptions. It's just that..." He paused, trying to backpedal and not having much luck. "Then why are you here?"

She flinched as if he'd struck her.

Damn, he should have handled that better. "I didn't mean to be a jerk. I guess my mood is only slightly better than it was the last time you saw me."

"You can say that again." She arched a brow then slowly shook her head.

"I owe you an apology for that day, too. But keep in mind that I'd just gotten the worst news of my life."

"You were also loaded down with pain medication, which can really take a toll on your thought process." Her downturned lips slowly curled into a pretty smile. "So you're forgiven."

He nodded, then pointed to the chair his mother had vacated. "Have a seat."

As she took the place beside him, she said, "I came to tell you something."

"What's that?"

She bit down on her bottom lip and paused for the longest time.

Finally, she said, "I'm pregnant."

ROCKING CHAIR RODEO:
Cowboys—and true love—never go out of style!

Dear Reader,

Last year, while visiting my son and his family on a military base, I had the opportunity to walk with the Stroller Warriors, a group of military spouses who meet at a park with their babies, toddlers and preschoolers. Then, while pushing strollers, they walk, jog or run to keep in shape while making friendships and providing support to each other.

One day, I was able to join the Stroller Warriors for a tour of a Black Hawk hangar. I got to sit in a helicopter and meet the pilots and crew. If you visit my website, I have photos posted. It was an amazing experience, and it provided me with the story idea for *The Soldier's Twin Surprise*.

After a romantic evening, Captain Clay Masters realizes that the beautiful brunette tourist he slept with is actually a sergeant at a nearby base. Fraternization with an enlisted soldier, albeit unintentional on both parts, is against regulations, so they reluctantly go their own ways—until Sergeant Erica Campbell learns she's pregnant—with twins!

It's not easy to face a pregnancy or parenthood alone, whether the other parent is deployed or absent for one reason or another. I was a single mom for a while and would love to connect with you on Facebook and share stories from the single mom or dad trenches.

In the meantime, I hope you'll enjoy my latest book in the Rocking Chair Rodeo series.

Happy reading!

Judy

PS: I love hearing from my readers. You can contact me through my website, judyduarte.com, or on Facebook: Facebook.com/judyduartenovelist.

The Soldier's Twin Surprise

Judy Duarte

HARLEQUIN® SPECIAL EDITION

If you purchased this book without a cover you should be aware that this book is stolen property. It was reported as "unsold and destroyed" to the publisher, and neither the author nor the publisher has received any payment for this "stripped book."

Recycling programs
for this product may
not exist in your area.

ISBN-13: 978-1-335-46587-0

The Soldier's Twin Surprise

Copyright © 2018 by Judy Duarte

All rights reserved. Except for use in any review, the reproduction or utilization of this work in whole or in part in any form by any electronic, mechanical or other means, now known or hereafter invented, including xerography, photocopying and recording, or in any information storage or retrieval system, is forbidden without the written permission of the publisher, Harlequin Enterprises Limited, 22 Adelaide St. West, 40th Floor, Toronto, Ontario M5H 4E3, Canada.

This is a work of fiction. Names, characters, places and incidents are either the product of the author's imagination or are used fictitiously, and any resemblance to actual persons, living or dead, business establishments, events or locales is entirely coincidental.

This edition published by arrangement with Harlequin Books S.A.

For questions and comments about the quality of this book, please contact us at CustomerService@Harlequin.com.

® and TM are trademarks of Harlequin Enterprises Limited or its corporate affiliates. Trademarks indicated with ® are registered in the United States Patent and Trademark Office, the Canadian Intellectual Property Office and in other countries.

Printed in U.S.A.

Since 2002, *USA TODAY* bestselling author **Judy Duarte** has written over forty books for Harlequin Special Edition, earned two RITA® Award nominations, won two Maggie Awards and received a National Readers' Choice Award. When she's not cooped up in her writing cave, she enjoys traveling with her husband and spending quality time with her grandchildren. You can learn more about Judy and her books on her website, judyduarte.com, or at Facebook.com/judyduartenovelist.

Books by Judy Duarte

Harlequin Special Edition

Rocking Chair Rodeo

Roping in the Cowgirl
The Bronc Rider's Baby
A Cowboy Family Christmas

The Fortunes of Texas: The Rulebreakers

No Ordinary Fortune

The Fortunes of Texas: The Secret Fortunes

From Fortune to Family Man

The Fortunes of Texas: All Fortune's Children

Wed by Fortune

Brighton Valley Cowboys

The Cowboy's Double Trouble
Having the Cowboy's Baby
The Boss, the Bride & the Baby

Visit the Author Profile page
at Harlequin.com for more titles.

To my son, Jeremy Colwell,
who serves as a medic in the United States Army.
I'm so proud of you and all you've accomplished.
You make this mom army proud.

Chapter One

If Captain Clay Masters hadn't been so focused on the sexy brunette wearing a red bikini, he might not have been nailed in the head by a spiraling football.

Damn. He glanced at his old high school buddies, both of whom were laughing like hell, and then he retrieved the ball.

Over the last thirteen years, he'd stayed in touch with Duck and Poncho via email, texts and occasional phone calls, but they hadn't spent any real time together since they'd all gone off to college. But you'd never know that. The moment they got together last Saturday in the baggage claim area of the Honolulu airport, it seemed as if they'd never gone their separate ways.

Now here they were, spending their well-earned vacation time on Oahu's North Shore. The surf season had ended weeks ago, so the beach was secluded and nearly empty, other than the three friends and the petite brunette stretched out on a towel on the sand.

Poncho nudged Clay's arm and nodded toward her. "She sure is rocking that red bikini."

He had that right. Clay hadn't been able to keep his eyes off her ever since she set out her towel on the sand. And when she'd applied her sunblock? He'd been tempted to ask if she wanted his help.

But he hadn't come here to hit on the first woman he saw. He wanted quality time with his buddies. Once they arrived, he'd traded in his flight suit for board shorts and flip-flops. He hadn't even bothered shaving the past two mornings, which gave him a shadow of a beard. And instead of answering to sir or Captain, he'd reverted to the nickname he'd earned as a star quarterback at Wexler High—Bullet.

"Remember what I told you when I picked you up at the airport," Clay told his buddies. "This week, I'm just a good ol' boy from Texas, soaking up the sun and enjoying the surf."

"We heard you," Poncho said. "But hell, Bullet, maybe you should reconsider and proclaim your military status. Just look at her."

Clay *had* been looking. She was stunning, with long brown hair and a body shaped to feminine perfection.

But ever since he'd gone to West Point, he'd been assigned to a military installation. And it hadn't mattered where he was stationed, there were always plenty of local women who wanted to latch on to a military man, particularly an officer, for the bragging rights. And the benefits package wasn't bad, either.

That didn't mean Clay hadn't had his share of romantic flings, but whenever he left the base, he usually kept his Army status under wraps.

"She looks lonely." Poncho nodded toward her. "I'm going to talk to her. Maybe she'd like to join us for a cold beer."

Duck laughed. "Just leave it to me, y'all. I've had more luck with the ladies than either of you."

"Maybe so, but she doesn't strike me as being your type." Clay stole another glance at the bikini-clad brunette. "She doesn't look like a buckle bunny or a rodeo queen."

At that, Poncho gave Duck a nudge. "Don't get carried away, man. She's got her eye on Bullet. I've seen her stealing peeks at him every so often."

Clay had noticed that, too, which was more than a little tempting. But he wasn't about to desert his friends, no matter how gorgeous a lady was. "Come on," he said. "This isn't supposed to be a week of nights on the prowl. We're here to relax and have fun—with each other. So are you going to stand around gawking at our neighbor or play ball?"

Poncho snatched the football from Clay's hands, and the game picked up right where they'd left off. But like before, Clay had a hell of a time keeping his focus on throwing passes. Or catching them.

"Hey, Bullet." Poncho slapped his hands on his hips. "You're lagging, old man."

Clay shook off his hormone-driven thoughts, realizing he'd gotten sluggish. So he threw a hard spiral to Poncho, who dropped it. "Ha! Look who's lagging now."

They continued to toss the ball, but how was Clay supposed to keep his mind on the game when he couldn't keep his eyes off the sexy brunette?

Finally, he decided to throw in the towel. So he called a time-out to his friends. "I'm ready for a cold beer." He was also ready to start the grill.

As his buddies trudged through the sand to the place where they'd left their stuff, two other young women, a blonde and a redhead, arrived at the shore and began setting out their ice chest and towels.

"What do you know," Poncho said. "Looks like we have company. And if Duck and I play our cards right, we could all get lucky tonight."

Poncho and Duck might be willing to sidle up to the newcomers, but Clay was still drawn to the olive-skinned brunette who could've modeled for the latest *Sports Illustrated* swimsuit issue. Not that she was doing anything especially sexy or alluring. Hell, she was just reading a book.

"It's clear that Clay has scoped out the brunette," Poncho said, "which is fine by me. I've always favored blondes. That is, unless Duck wants to arm wrestle me for her."

"No problem," Duck said. "I'll take the redhead."

"Okay, guys." Clay folded his arms across his chest. "What if they're not interested?"

"Oh, they're interested. They keep looking over here and giggling. But you'll have to work a little magic on the brunette." Poncho chuckled. "Something tells me you've gotten a little rusty at laying on the charm."

"I've still got the touch. There are some things a guy doesn't forget." But Clay wasn't in the mood for romantic fun and games tonight, especially if his friends struck out with the new arrivals. In fact, he had half a notion to go back to their rented beach house, open a cold one, turn on the TV and hang out inside. Alone.

"While you light the grill," Poncho told Duck, "I'll lay a little *buenos días* on the lovely twosome and invite them to our barbecue." Then he glanced at Clay. "What are you waiting for? Go offer the brunette an invite. Or would you rather I lay a little groundwork for you first?"

"I don't need your help." Clay stole another glance at the brunette. Chances were, she was on vacation, too.

Oh, what the hell. He supposed it wouldn't hurt to talk to her. Maybe she'd be interested in the cowboy type and in sharing a night they'd both remember— long after they each went their own ways.

Sergeant Erica Campbell lay on her back, her open historical romance novel held up to shield her eyes from the sun's glare while she read.

Earlier this afternoon, she'd noticed the three hotties who'd been splashing in the water and playing football on the shore. The one called Bullet had glanced her way, and when their eyes met, he tossed her a big, Texas-size grin. She meant to ignore him, but he seemed so boyish and charming that she couldn't help returning his smile.

All three of them were attractive and well built, but

Bullet either spent a lot of time at the gym or had a job that required strength and vigor.

His light brown hair was short, much like his friends'. Water glistened on his broad shoulders. Six-pack abs and a taut belly drew her undivided attention like a sharp, crisp salute. Now there was a real hunk. And a drop-dead gorgeous one at that.

But the last thing she needed to do, especially this weekend, was to give someone the idea that she wanted company. So she quickly averted her gaze, reached into her small tote bag for the spray bottle of sunblock and applied it. Then she lay back down on the towel and reached for her novel.

Male laughter erupted yet again, drawing her from her story as it had several times since she'd come outside her rented beachfront bungalow to catch a few rays. As much as she'd wanted to ignore the three men who were sharing the same stretch of beach with her, she found that next to impossible. Two of them had a slight southern drawl, and she suspected they were Texas natives, just as she was. One of them also appeared to be Latino. So was she, although she couldn't speak a lick of Spanish.

Their short haircuts suggested they might be in the military. That wouldn't be unusual. There were quite a few bases located on the island.

She made it a point to avoid men stationed on Oahu, even though that wasn't easy. Men often approached her, even when she was in uniform, and tried to hit on her. So the bikini she was wearing today was a little risky, since it might draw even more attention to her.

It's not that she was stuck-up or prudish, but she'd witnessed firsthand how deployments and conflicting duty assignments could take their toll on a relationship, especially when both people were in the military.

She loved being stationed in Honolulu. She didn't much like being downtown in Waikiki, though. It was too much like other big cities. But the North Shore, as far as she was concerned, was paradise on earth.

Again, she glanced at the handsome tourists. They seemed to be in their late twenties or early thirties. And they shared a playful camaraderie she found interesting.

Listening to their conversation, she'd picked up on their nicknames. She and her sister Elena had done the same thing, calling themselves Rickie and Lainie when they were girls. She wondered if they would have continued doing that until adulthood. Probably. They'd been so close. And for the most part, they'd only had each other.

As the guys teased each other about a dirt-bike crash that resulted in Bullet getting a gash in his head and Poncho puking at the sight of blood, she realized they'd grown up together. That they'd been friends for a long time.

She wished she'd kept in contact with some of her high school friends, but when she enlisted nearly six years ago, she'd lost touch with them. Not that she hadn't made new ones. It's just that the Army had a way of shaking things up with regular deployments or reassignments.

Again, the three laughed at something that had landed them in detention, further convincing her that they were high school buddies who'd come to Hawaii on vacation. Not that it mattered. Erica wasn't here to gawk at hot guys. She was here to think, to regroup and to kick that shadow of guilt she felt as she grieved for her adoptive parents.

She'd cried when she'd gotten the news of the accident and then again at the funeral. She'd loved them. How could she not? They'd rescued her from the foster care system when she'd been in the third grade.

Still, it had taken a long time for her to bond with the couple. But that was probably due to the hospitalization and the death of her twin sister that same year. Now there was a crushing loss that had struck hard, leaving a void that would never go away.

Needless to say, the Army was Erica's family now. And in a couple of months, when her contract was up, she'd eagerly reenlist without giving it a second thought.

She'd just reached an especially steamy part of her novel when a shadow crossed her face, drawing her from the heated love scene. She assumed the sun had passed behind a cloud until a man cleared his throat.

Startled, she glanced up. When she spotted one of the guys standing over her, the hottie she'd heard them call Bullet, she slammed the book shut and set it aside with the cover facedown. Her cheeks, already warmed by the sun, as well as the words on the page, heated to the boiling point.

Talk about getting caught red-handed—or rather red faced! Had he realized she'd been in the middle of a love scene?

"I'm sorry," Bullet said. "I didn't mean to surprise you or interrupt your reading."

She sat up and combed her fingers through her hair. "You have nothing to be sorry about. That book wasn't very good anyway. I was just about to throw it into the ocean."

"I could do that for you," he said. "I've got a pretty good arm."

"So I noticed. I assume that's why they call you Bullet."

His lips quirked into a crooked grin, and he gave a little shrug.

Arrogant guys were a real turnoff. Usually. But she loved football and found this particular quarterback intriguing. But there was no way in hell she'd hand over that blasted book to him. And even though she'd claimed otherwise, it had been a great story, one she intended to finish, although that wasn't going to happen this afternoon.

Neither of them spoke, and as he studied her, she felt vulnerable. And half-dressed. If her swimsuit cover-up was handy, she'd slip it on now.

She blamed the self-consciousness on that damn love scene, but in all honesty, Bullet wasn't making it easy to forget the words she'd read. The bare chest. The heated kiss. The hand slipping into the slick, silky folds...

"You on vacation?" he asked.

She rarely shared intimate details about herself with strangers, but the guy seemed like a friendly sort. So she nodded and said, "Yes." She had to report at the base before midnight on Sunday.

"My buddies and I are checking out on Sunday morning," Bullet said.

She used her hand to shield the afternoon sun from her eyes. "I noticed your accents. Are you guys from Texas?"

"Yep. We grew up in Wexler. It's in south Texas, about two hours from Houston. Ever hear of it?"

"Actually, I have. I was born in Houston and went to high school in Jeffersville, which is about fifty miles from there."

"No kidding? Small world."

"In some ways." But it could be a great big world, too. And lonely.

Bullet swept a muscular arm toward the water. "How 'bout that ocean? Ever see anything that blue?"

"It's amazing, isn't it?" In fact, that's why she spent a lot of her free time at the beach on the North Shore.

"You here with friends?" he asked.

"Not at the moment." She glanced at the two women sitting together on a blanket in the sand. It might be nice to have someone with her today, someone to offer solace and a diversion. But she didn't.

"Just spending some alone time?" he asked.

She didn't see a need to reveal that she was staying by herself this weekend, although she was pretty damn good at defending herself—with a gun or in hand-to-hand combat. "I have two vacation days left,, so I rented that bungalow behind me."

"That makes us neighbors." Bullet nodded toward his friends, who'd stopped playing and now stood with their hands on their hips, talking to two other women who'd just arrived. "We're staying in the house next door."

She'd already come to that conclusion, but she didn't comment.

"We're going to be grilling brats and hot dogs," Bullet added. "And we've got plenty of beer on ice. Sodas, too. We even have a bottle of vodka and some OJ. You're welcome to join us."

Erica looked at his buddies, her gaze returning to Bullet, her attraction growing by leaps and bounds.

"Just so you know," he added, "my friends and I are nice guys. Trustworthy and honorable. Especially Poncho. His day job is driving a squad car down Wexler's main drag, keeping the residents safe."

One of them was a police officer? She hadn't expected that.

Erica was usually skeptical of flirtatious men, but something told her Bullet was honest. And that she'd be safe with the three Texas tourists.

So in spite of her plan to spend the rest of the day and evening alone, she agreed to join them.

"We'll be starting the grill soon," Bullet said. "How does an ice-cold beer sound?"

Every bit of common sense she'd ever had prompted her to say that she'd reconsidered, that she was going to pass on the barbecue after all. She wasn't especially fond of hot dogs. But the loneliness and grief were getting to her, so she felt compelled to say, "Sure. Why not?"

"I'll bring a beer over to you," he said. "Unless you'd prefer a soda or mixed drink? I could make you a screwdriver."

"Actually, the beer is fine."

"You got it." Then he turned and walked away, gracing her with a view of his broad shoulders and swim trunks that rode low on narrow hips and outlined a great pair of glutes. Dang. The guy had a heart-stopping swagger.

Moments later, after she'd shoved the novel into her tote bag and brushed out her hair, he returned with two ice-cold longnecks and handed one to her. She looked at the label. It was the Longboard Island Lager, made by the Kona Brewing Company. Apparently, these guys wanted the whole Hawaii experience.

"Mind if I sit here?" he asked.

"Go ahead." She moved the ice chest, making room for him to sit beside her on the towel.

Instead, he chose the sand. She appreciated the humble move. She hated it when men tried to push boundaries. And the fact that Bullet seemed a bit shy and cordial was a bit of a turn-on.

Who was she kidding? It was more than a little alluring.

She took a long, refreshing drink. It had taken her a while to get used to the taste of beer, but after some time in the Army, she'd come to enjoy it after a hard day in the field.

"Tell me something," she said. "Honestly. Is Poncho really a cop?"

"Yep. In fact, he was just promoted to detective."

"I suppose he looks more like an authority figure in his uniform."

Bullet laughed. "I don't blame you for being surprised. Poncho used to be the rowdy one who led me and Duck astray, but once he turned twenty-one, he shocked the entire town, if not the high school, by joining the Wexler Police Department."

"And Duck?" she asked. "Is he in law enforcement, too?"

"No, he'd rather be a lawbreaker."

"Seriously?"

Bullet chuckled. "Maybe back in our high school days, but not so much anymore. Actually, he's a rodeo cowboy. And a good one."

She tended to be skeptical by nature, especially of men she'd just met, but Duck had a soft Texas twang and a lanky, muscular build. Of course, looks could be deceiving. Yet something in Bullet's eyes suggested he wasn't giving her a line of bull.

"What about you?" she asked, more curious about Bullet than the others.

He didn't answer right away, then offered her a charming smile that dimpled his lightly bristled cheeks and made him appear both rugged and boyish at the same time. "Let's just say that I can outride, out rope and outshoot both of them."

That surprised her, although she wasn't sure why it would. And he'd admitted that he was a better cowboy than the others, which just might be true. At least he hadn't bragged about the number of silver belt buckles he'd won in the rodeo.

Erica had pretty much outgrown the type of guys she'd known as a teenager back in Jeffersville. Nevertheless, she found Bullet far more attractive than she should.

"How long will you be in Hawaii?" Bullet asked. Erica wasn't about to reveal too many personal details with a guy she'd just met, no matter how hunky he was or how trustworthy she thought he might be. But then again, she didn't see any reason not to be somewhat honest. If she kept the story simple, he wouldn't have enough information about her to find her again—if he turned out to be a jerk. He didn't need to know that she was stationed in Honolulu for the time being.

"Actually," she said, "I just flew in from Houston." It was the truth, of course. And it supported her comment about having two days left of her vacation. But she'd actually just returned from bereavement leave.

Several weeks ago, she'd gotten an early-morning call from the Texas hospital where her parents had been taken after the accident. Her father had suffered a massive coronary while driving home from church. The car had crashed through a guardrail and rolled down an embankment. He was pronounced dead on arrival, and her mom died from her injuries a few hours later.

Erica sucked in a deep breath and slowly blew it out. It had been a long month, a sad and lonely one. She'd gone to Texas to bury the parents who'd adopted her.

But the worst was past. She had two days left of her leave before she had to report to duty at Schofield Barracks, so she'd rented the bungalow through Airbnb, where she hoped the warm sun, the soft tropical breeze and the sound of waves lapping on the sand would provide a healing balm.

She and Bullet sat there awhile, both caught up in their own thoughts. Or so it seemed.

"What's your name?" he asked.

She could have told him anything at that point—Jennifer, Heather, Alexis. She'd heard that it was a game some women played. They'd create fake careers and backgrounds, too. But Erica wouldn't go that far. Instead, since he and his friends referred to each other with nicknames, she'd offer him one, too. The one her twin sister had given her years ago. "My name is Rickie."

He nodded, as if making a mental note, then took a chug of beer. Since he hadn't offered up his real name, she didn't ask. What was the point? She didn't expect to see him after she checked out and returned to base.

It was weird, though. She hadn't been called Rickie since the night Lainie had gone to the hospital for the surgery that failed. At the memory, at the thought of the final words they'd shared with each other, a pang of grief shot through her, reminding her that she'd lost her entire family. Two of them, in fact. Not many people could claim to be orphaned twice, but this time around, at twenty-five, it was a lot easier than when she and Lainie had been eight.

Under the circumstances, she probably should keep to herself tonight so she could dwell on her emotions and come up with a good game plan to face the future. Wasn't that why she'd come to North Shore this weekend?

For someone determined to keep to herself, she couldn't explain why she'd let herself be enticed by the hunky, football-playing tourists. Maybe it was some sort of coping mechanism preventing her from dealing with her own issues, her own sadness.

If she could distract herself with the antics of a trio of strangers reliving their glory days on the beach, then she wouldn't be forced to think about her recent loss.

But she'd much rather laugh than cry. And these guys were playful and entertaining. Intriguing and handsome. Especially Bullet. Besides, she didn't have to tell him that she was in the Army and actually lived nearby.

Why get so personal when, after Sunday morning, she'd never see him again?

Chapter Two

By the time the sun went down, and a couple of automatic porch lights from the nearby beach house kicked on, Clay's buddies had moved closer to the blonde and the redhead. But Clay was right where he wanted to be, sitting on the sand and enjoying a second cold beer with Rickie. Things seemed to have clicked between them, which was a little surprising.

He hadn't planned to hook up with any women this week, but he also hadn't expected Rickie to be so easy to talk to. She was a little on the quiet side, but she was bright. And her laugh, which he'd only heard a time or two, had a mesmerizing lilt.

Hey. The night was still young…

Of course, that didn't mean he wasn't being realistic. She'd be returning to her life in Texas soon, and after he drove his buddies to the airport Sunday morning, he'd head back to Wheeler Army Airfield. Still, that left them thirty-six hours. More or less.

"Are you ready for another beer?" he asked.

She looked at her nearly empty bottle. "No, I think I'll switch to soda—if you have any left."

Clay got up, headed for the ice chest and retrieved two cans—one cola and a lemon-lime. Then he took a moment to walk to the grassy area near their beach house, where Duck had set up the small grill about fifteen minutes earlier. The coals were coming along okay.

He glanced over at his buddies. Duck, who'd just said something to make the redhead laugh, glanced up and caught Clay's eye. Clay nodded at the grill, gave him the thumbs-up sign and returned to Rickie.

He offered her both cans. "Take your pick."

She chose the cola. "Thanks."

"We'll be putting those dogs on the grill soon," he said. "Are you getting hungry?"

"A little." She scanned the beach, her gaze landing on the others, who'd moved over to the grassy area, near the grill and within the perimeter of light coming from the porch. "You know, even though I said I'd join you guys tonight, I'm not really in the mood for a party."

Neither was Clay. In fact, he'd rather sit here all evening, enjoying what little time he and Rickie had left. "Why don't I bring over a couple of hot dogs for us once they're cooked?"

"That'd be nice. Thanks." She made a little hole in the sand, one big enough to hold the bottom of her can. Once she set it down, she turned to him and blessed him with a pretty smile. "So what was it like growing up in Wexler?"

"I doubt it was much different from your neck of the woods. I lived on a ranch, though. So I had a lot of chores to do each day, plus a cow to milk and a couple of chickens to feed."

"That's cool. I never had any pets."

Clay wouldn't call an old milk cow or four harpy hens pets.

"Do you still live in Wexler?" she asked.

"No, after high school I moved on." He nearly added, *to bigger and better things*, but there was no reason to share his West Point experience. And his military career was still off the table.

"Do you miss it?" she asked.

"The ranch? No, not at all." He didn't consider himself a small-town boy anymore. He was a soldier now. And Army proud.

"When I was in high school, I lived on a quiet street in Jeffersville," she said. "The houses were all two-story and pretty similar, except we were the only ones who had a pool in our backyard. Actually, I guess I still have one."

The comment struck him as a little odd. "So you live with your parents?"

"No, they both passed away recently. In a car accident. So the house belongs to me now."

"I'm sorry. That must have been tough."

She shrugged. "It was, but I'm dealing with it."

He was about to say something, but the shadow that touched her gaze passed faster than a ghost, so he let it go at that. He didn't want to stir up any sad memories for her.

Apparently, she didn't want to dwell on them, either, because, after a couple of beats, she asked, "Does your family still live on that ranch?"

"My mom does. My dad died when I was young. When I was a teenager, she and I moved in with my paternal grandfather and my step-grandfather."

Rickie turned toward him, her knee drawn up and bent, her hands clasped around her shin. "Tell me about her."

"Who? My mom?" He hadn't seen *that* coming.

"Yes, I'm curious about her. My real mother died when I was really young, so I never had the chance to know her."

"I thought you said your parents died recently."

"They did. I was orphaned the first time when I was eight and then adopted when I was nine." She cast a glance his way. When their eyes met, she seemed to reel him into her story. Into her life. "My adoptive mother was good to me, but she wasn't very maternal. At least, not the way I imagined a mom should be. Know what I mean?"

Not really. But he nodded just the same.

"I'm not complaining. It's just that I had a super-cool foster mom once." She seemed to brighten from the memory, rebounding easily, which was a relief. Clay didn't like the sad, pensive look that had touched her expression a few moments ago.

Hoping to prolong the happier thoughts, he asked, "What was cool about her?"

"Pretty much everything." Rickie's smile deepened,

her mood transformed. "Her name was Mama Kate—at least, that's what we called her. I have no idea how old she was. Probably in her sixties. She was heavyset with an easy laugh and a loving heart. She never turned down a kid needing placement, so her house was packed with children. Yet she always found special time for each of us. And she was a whiz in the kitchen. She made the best meals—healthy and tasty at the same time. And her cookie jar was always full."

Clay's mom was a good cook, too, although she didn't do much baking anymore. At least, he didn't think she did. It had been a long time since he'd seen her face-to-face. They talked on the phone, of course. Usually on Sundays. But he didn't go home too often. Just for Christmas—and only if he wasn't deployed or stationed too far away.

"How long did you get to live with Mama Kate?" he asked.

"Not long enough."

She didn't explain, but Clay sensed a sadness about her. Without a conscious thought, he reached out and placed his hand on her bent knee, offering his comfort and support. Or maybe he just wanted an opportunity to touch her.

"It sounds like Mama Kate set a good example for you," he said.

Rickie smiled, and this time, when their eyes met, something warm surged between them. If he didn't know better, he'd think they'd made some kind of emotional connection, one that might linger indefinitely. But they really hadn't. How could they? They'd just met. And they'd never see each other again.

Yet the longer they sat in the soft glow emanating from the porch lights, the more surreal the evening seemed. Sure, Rickie was just as pretty, just as sexy as ever, but there was so much more to her. And if she lived around here…

But she didn't.

Reluctantly, he removed his hand from her knee. "I grew up without a father, but my granddad tried to set a pretty good example for me. He was tough as nails, but he also had a soft side."

Again, she smiled. "So you grew up with a lot of love."

"Too much at times."

Her brow furrowed. "What do you mean?"

"My mom was one of those helicopter parents. She hovered over me, hell-bent on keeping me safe, close to home and under her wing."

At that, Rickie drew up both knees. Her smile deepened, sparking something in her pretty brown eyes. It felt pretty damn good to think that he'd done or said something that had caused her pleasure. But for some reason, he didn't want her to get the wrong idea about him or his mother.

"You might think that's cool," he said, "but you have no idea how tough it was to live with a mom like mine. Our relationship was pretty strained most of the time, which caused me to rebel every chance I got."

Rickie cocked her head to the side, causing her curls to tumble over her shoulder. He was tempted to reach out, to touch them, to see if they were just as soft as they looked. But this time, he kept his hand to himself.

"In what ways did you rebel?" she asked.

He thought for a moment, wanting to choose the right example to share. For some dumb reason, he didn't want to tell her about the time he and Duck got caught drinking Granddad's Jack Daniel's behind the barn. Or when he and Poncho lit up cigars in the old lot near the ball field and set the dried grass on fire.

"When I was just a little kid," he said, "maybe four or five years old, my grandparents came to visit. It was right before Halloween, and Granddad's wife made me a purple superhero cape to go with my costume. Even days after I'd gone trick-or-treating, I wore that silly thing all the time. And whenever I'd see my mom standing at the kitchen sink and gazing out the window, I'd climb one of the nearby trees and jump out of it. I knew I couldn't really fly, but I'd pretend to. And my mom would really freak out."

"Surely you don't blame her for doing that. You could have broken your neck."

"Yeah, I know. But she used to hit the roof about a lot of things. And the older I got, the more protective she seemed to get. I can't tell you how many camping trips I missed because she couldn't go and didn't want to let me out of her sight." Clay took a sip of his cola, wishing he'd gotten another beer instead.

"I'm surprised she let you play football," Rickie said.

He laughed. "I grew up in Texas. We love high school football."

"You're damn straight," Rickie said. "*Friday Night Lights* and all of that. Did your mom go to your games?"

"Hell, she sat in the front row for every single one. And once, when I was sacked especially hard, she ran out on the field to make sure I was okay. The coach had to tell her to back off and return to the bleachers."

Again there went that pretty, heart-strumming smile that lit her honey-colored eyes. "Your poor mom."

"Maybe so. But she would have been better off having a girl." One like Rickie, who would have enjoyed baking cookies with her or sitting in a cozy chair reading storybooks. A girly-girl who wouldn't mind sticking around the house all day instead of messing around with the guys and getting ready to jump on any wild-ass idea that Clay or his friends thought would be fun and exciting.

"Hey, Bullet!"

At the sound of Poncho's voice, Clay looked over his shoulder to see his buddy manning the grill. The ladies had moved over to the grassy area, too. And from the looks of it, the evening's festivities had begun.

"The hot dogs are just about ready," Poncho called out. "Come and get 'em."

"I'll bring a couple of plates back for us," Clay told Rickie.

When he returned, one plate was loaded with hot dogs. The other held a couple of paper cups filled with condiments.

"Oh my gosh." Rickie laughed. "Who do you expect to eat all of that?"

He shrugged. "I thought you'd want more than one."

"No, I'm not very hungry—or a big fan of food that comes wrapped in a bun."

He handed her the empty plate. She took it, then reached for a hot dog from the stack. When he sat beside her, this time sitting on the edge of her towel, he asked, "So what kind of food *do* you like?"

"Anything served in a tortilla."

"Tacos and burritos, huh? I like Mexican food, too." Clay reached for a hot dog, just as Duck turned up his iPod, which he'd programmed with all his favorite country-western tunes.

"Ooh," Rickie said. "I love Toby Keith."

"Me, too. Apparently we have a lot in common."

"We do?"

Clay nodded. "We both grew up in small Texas towns. And we like football, Mexican food and country-western music."

"That's true," she said.

Rickie was a girl after his own heart—at least for the rest of the weekend. He was batting a thousand when it came to finding things to like and admire about a woman he wasn't ever going to see again.

Yet that didn't matter. Not on a night like this. Maybe it was the tropical breeze, the moonlight glistening on the water or the soft sounds of a sultry ballad that played in the background.

Hell, maybe it was her. Or just him.

Whatever it was, the air was filled with sexual promise.

A glance at his buddies proved that. They'd already formed couples.

Had Rickie noticed? Was she feeling it, too?

As another tune began to play, something alluring and suggestive, Clay cut a glance at Rickie and tried to read her mood. She was still seated, but she'd closed her eyes and was gently swaying to the music.

Clay got to his feet, and when she looked up at him, he held out his hand. "Dance with me."

Her lips parted, and for a moment, he thought she was going to decline. But she surprised him by slipping her hand in his and letting him draw her to her feet, away from the light—and the others.

Clay couldn't believe his luck. He'd wanted to get his hands on Rickie ever since he first laid eyes on her, and now he was dancing with her in the sand.

She felt so good in his arms. Their swimsuits left little to the imagination and didn't provide much of a barrier, so he held her skin to skin.

The coconut scent of her sunblock mingled with the tropical fragrance of her shampoo, something floral. It was an interesting combination. And intoxicating.

Her breasts, soft and full, pressed against his chest, and her cheek rested on his shoulder. But they weren't just swaying to the music, lulled by the beat. There was a lot more than that going on. Pheromones filled the night air, and his hormones were pumped and at the ready.

He ran his hands along her back and over the tiny bow she'd tied to hold her bikini top in place. It wouldn't take much to remove it. Just a little tug on one of the strings.

It might be a tempting thought, but it wasn't one he'd

put into action. Instead, he continued to caress her sun-kissed skin until he came dangerously close to the small piece of red fabric that barely covered her lovely back-side. It took all he had to refrain from moving lower, from stroking her…

Watch yourself, man. Don't ruin the moment.

He wished it would last forever, but it wouldn't. Min-utes from now, the last chords of this song would fade. Then they'd return to where they'd been sitting in the sand. Or maybe Rickie would say good-night and leave him out here alone.

If that happened, he'd deal with it. Like they said, all good things must come to an end.

And then they did. All too quickly. The music that followed the love song had a lively beat, one that lent itself to a Texas two-step. Something better suited for a crowded dance floor on a rip-roaring Saturday night than a moonlit tropical beach.

Rickie was the first to draw away, breaking their embrace and dashing the romantic mood—until Clay took a close look at her face in the soft amber glow of a distant porch light.

When she looked up at him and smiled, his body hardened with desire for her, and he damn near stopped breathing.

"What do you think?" she asked. "Should we take this inside?"

"Good idea."

Granted, she might only be suggesting that they go indoors, turn on her favorite playlist and dance in private, but right now, with his hormones raging, he'd follow her anywhere.

She took him by the hand, led him across the grass and to the front of the bungalow. After opening the door, she stepped inside and flipped on the light switch. He followed her in.

He still wasn't sure what she had in mind until she crossed the room, headed for the sliding glass door that provided a beach view and drew the shutters, securing their privacy.

Apparently, they were both on the same page. He scanned the single room that provided a sitting area, a kitchen and a double bed. It was small, but nice. Clean and cozy.

He took a moment to check out the simple island decor, the framed surf posters, a watercolor of a sailboat on the high seas, a display of conch shells on a shelf near the wall-mounted television.

"This place is pretty small," Rickie said, "but big enough for me."

She'd implied earlier that someone might join her here. He suspected she hadn't wanted him to think she was all alone. But apparently, she felt comfortable with him now.

She closed the distance between them and studied his face, his mouth. She lifted her index finger and wiggled it at him. "You have a smidge of mustard on your lip. Do you mind if I...?"

He probably ought to be embarrassed and swipe his hand across his face to remove any smears or brush off a lingering crumb, but he longed for her to touch him. "Go ahead."

She placed her finger against the side of his mouth and gave it a little rub. If he had anything there, it wasn't much.

As her hand lowered, he reached for her wrist and held it firm. "I'm not sure where this is heading, Rickie, but I know where I'd like it to go."

She gazed at him for a couple of beats before tossing him a breezy smile. "Looks like we're both in agreement."

He could have swept her into his arms right then and there, but it wasn't that easy. He released her wrist. "There's only one problem. I don't have any condoms."

She bit down on her bottom lip and furrowed her brow, apparently stymied by their dilemma.

He supposed they could walk into town and look for a drugstore. But that was going to put a big damper on the mood.

Suddenly, she brightened. "I just remembered. I have one in my overnight bag."

"Then we're in luck." And not just because of the condom. Rickie was a sexy little package, and he was glad she was prepared.

"I've had it for a while," she confessed. "I don't make a habit of inviting men home."

He believed her. And somehow that made tonight even more special. He opened his arms, and she stepped into his embrace. As she wrapped her arms around his neck and pressed their nearly naked bodies together, he cupped her jaw and drew her lips to his.

The kiss began sweet, but within a heartbeat, it deepened. She opened her mouth, allowing his tongue to mate with hers, dipping, twisting and tasting as if they were so hungry they'd never get their fill.

He let his hands slip along her neck, to her shoulders and down to her waist, where he stroked her skin and explored her curves. When he reached her breast, his thumb skimmed against the red fabric, across a taut nipple, and her breath caught. A surge of desire shot right through him. With one hand still kneading her breast, he used the other to reach around to her backside, cup her bottom and pull her close, against his erection.

She pressed back, rubbing against him and heightening his arousal until he was tempted to lift her into his arms and carry her to bed. But before he had the chance, she ended the kiss.

"I'd better go find my tote bag. We're going to need that condom." She strode across the room and to the sofa, where a blue canvas bag rested, and reached inside. Moments later, she turned to him with a smile, holding the small packet like a prize. "Got it!"

Silently thanking whatever island god was looking out for them, he took her by the hand and led her to the bed. She placed the condom on the small nightstand. Then she reached behind her back, removed her skimpy bikini top and dropped it to the floor. As she peeled off the tiny bottom piece, his gaze never left her.

If he'd thought she was gorgeous before, he found her flat-out breathtaking now, standing before him in all her naked glory. Feminine perfection at its finest. And tonight, she was his.

Following her lead, he slipped off his board shorts, then joined her on the double bed and eased toward her, determined to please her and to make sure she wouldn't have any regrets in the morning. He sure as hell wouldn't. Not when their chemistry was off the charts.

She reached for the packet and handed it to him. He tore it open. Once he'd protected them both, she reached for his erection, opened for him and guided him home.

Okay, not *home*. That sounded too permanent, too lasting. This was a temporary relationship, a fling, one that was as short-term as a beachfront vacation rental. Here today, gone tomorrow.

He shook off the stray thought as he entered her. As he thrust deep, her body responded to his. She arched up, matching the tempo, creating their own.

As she reached a peak, she cried out and let go. He shuddered, releasing with her in a sexual explosion, their very own display of fireworks. He almost wished the rush could last forever—

No, *not* forever. This was just a one-night deal—or, hopefully, two. He'd have to make a drugstore run first thing in the morning and purchase a box of condoms. They'd never have the time to use them all before they said goodbye on Sunday morning and went their own ways. But after what they'd just shared, he suspected they'd need quite a few.

Erica never slept with anyone on the first date, let alone the first *meet*. But she'd been through a lot in the past month, suffered a tragic loss. And for some crazy reason, she'd wanted to feel a connection to another human being. To be held. To be…

Well, she didn't expect to find love or anything like that. But she'd thought it would be nice to feel liked, valued and appreciated.

And wow. She'd gotten so much better than that.

She wasn't a virgin, but neither would she consider herself to be sexually experienced. That was, until tonight. Bullet had taken her to a place she'd never been before—and one she feared she'd never go again.

She felt beautiful. Special. Adored.

Their lovemaking had turned her world on its axis—in a good way. While basking in his arms during a stunning afterglow, she'd been able to forget the funeral, the grief, the meetings with her parents' attorney, the house that needed a slew of repairs before she could sell it or find renters.

But more than that, she'd found herself reevaluating the future.

Not her decision to reenlist, of course. That wouldn't happen. She'd found strength and courage in the Army. She also had a sense of pride in herself and her accomplishments. There was no way she'd go back to Texas and to the small-town life she'd once known.

But that didn't mean she couldn't see Bullet again. Maybe visit him sometime. She might even be able to spend her next leave with him in Texas.

Of course, she had no idea how he'd feel about seeing *her* again after this weekend. Either way, a future together didn't seem likely. Not many men would want to follow their wives from base to base.

Okay, so she was putting the proverbial cart before the horse. Their heartbeats had barely slowed to normal, and they'd yet to say a word about what they'd just done, let alone discuss what might come next.

So she continued to lie with him, cuddling in bed with their legs entwined. But she wasn't ready to move, unless it was closer to Bullet.

When he pressed a kiss on her brow, she finally spoke. "That was amazing."

"I couldn't agree more."

She'd hoped he'd say that, although she had every reason to believe he felt the same way she did.

"I could stay here forever," she said, then wished she could reel in her words. She hadn't meant to overstep or to imply something that might frighten him off. So she added a bit of a disclaimer. "I meant stay here on the North Shore. In this cute little bungalow. And if I didn't have to go back to work, I'd stay in bed with you."

He stroked her shoulder, which suggested he hadn't let her comment bother him.

What would he say if she suggested they meet up in Texas in the near future? She could take personal leave so she could find renters after the handyman had made the repairs to the house. Up until now, she'd planned to hire a property manager so she wouldn't have to do it herself.

Still, if she oversaw things on her own, she could look up Bullet. Would he be up for something like that?

He said he no longer lived on the family ranch in Wexler, but he hadn't mentioned where he lived now. So it might not work out the way she thought it would.

Actually, there was a lot she didn't know about him. It hadn't mattered earlier, but it did now. She supposed they'd have to talk about stuff like that.

She glanced at the clock on the nightstand. Did they have time for that kind of discussion now? Or should she let it go until morning? She propped herself up on her elbow and glanced over Bullet's shoulder to get a better look.

Apparently, he must have realized what she was attempting to do, because he asked, "What time is it?"

"Almost twenty-one hundred."

He stiffened. "What'd you say?"

"I'm sorry." She sighed softly. "Military time comes naturally to me."

He didn't respond right away, but the muscles in his arm seemed pretty tight.

"Were you in the military?" he asked.

"Actually, I still am." She supposed it wouldn't hurt to lay her cards on the table, to have that little talk now. "I'm going to make a career of it. Why?"

His biceps twitched. "Something tells me we just came to a place where the old don't-ask-don't-tell line would be appropriate."

Uh-oh. Now it was her turn to stiffen.

"What branch of the service are you in?" he asked.

A sense of foreboding crossed her mind, and her heart hammered in her chest as if trying to break through her rib cage. "I'm in the Army."

He inhaled deeply, then slowly blew it out. "Where are you stationed?"

"Schofield Barracks. Does that matter?"

"It might."

Oh, for Pete's sake. Surely he wasn't in the Army, too. If so, was he stationed in Texas? But wait, that's not what he'd said. Was it?

She rolled away and practically shot up in bed. Then she folded her arms across her chest and turned to him. "You lied to me. You're not a cowboy from Texas."

"I grew up on a ranch in Wexler, and I've ridden plenty of horses over the years. But I never claimed to be a cowboy."

"So you're in the Army, too?" she asked, dreading the response.

"Yeah, I am. And apparently, I wasn't the only one to withhold some details over the last few hours."

"I *am* on vacation," she said. "But only until tomorrow night, when I have to check in at the base."

Bullet sat up and scrubbed his hand over his hair. *Please don't let him be an officer.* It was against regulations to fraternize.

That sense of foreboding grew, casting a shadow over her. Over them.

"What's your rank?" he asked.

"You go first."

Bullet swore under his breath. "I'm Captain Clayton Masters. I command a Black Hawk squadron on Wheeler Army Airfield. And you're…?"

Rickie blew out a sigh, plopped back down on the mattress and placed her hands over her face. "Sergeant Erica Campbell—enlisted."

What rotten luck. Her lover wasn't a cowboy from Texas. Nor was he a tourist on vacation.

Instead, he was a Black Hawk commander. An officer in the US Army.

And they'd just fraternized.

It hadn't been intentional. And as long as they didn't do it again, she supposed it was no big deal.

"I guess we screwed up," Bullet said. "Ah, no pun intended."

She blew out a weary sigh. "Big-time. If I'd known who you were, I never would have invited you back here."

"And if I'd known who *you* were, I wouldn't have come."

"I never expected more than one night anyway," Rickie said, although, just moments ago, she'd begun to hope for more. To wonder how they could possibly pull that off. "So no harm, no foul. Right?"

"That's what I'm thinking." Bullet—or rather, Clay—raked a hand through his hair. A military cut, she now realized.

Damn. Should she call him *Captain*? After what they'd done, that felt awkward.

"I guess we really are neighbors," he said, as he got to his feet and reached for his discarded board shorts.

"That's about the size of it." Wheeler Airfield was just across the street from Schofield Barracks.

Rickie figured she'd better get dressed, too, and climbed out of bed. Rather than put on her swimsuit, she rummaged through her suitcase and pulled out a green T-shirt and a pair of black shorts. She wouldn't bother with a bra or panties.

"What's your MOS?" he asked, referring to her military occupation specialty.

"I'm a sixty-eight whiskey."

"So you're a medic."

"I work at a clinic unless I'm sent out for training ops." And those often began on Wheeler, especially when she and her unit had to fly out to the Big Island. Damn, what a disappointing—not to mention *awkward*—mess this was turning out to be.

She slipped into her clothes, covering herself quickly as if they could pretend none of this happened. But good luck with that. The sex had been too damn good to forget.

"I suppose that means we could run into each other."

True. So far, she hadn't been on any missions with him, although she could. The Black Hawks usually flew soldiers out to the Big Island, where a lot of training took place. And since he was the commander of a squadron, it could happen in the future.

Yep. Definitely awkward.

"You know," he said, "we can't do this again."

She wasn't stupid, although she felt like it. "I've never done this before—made love with a guy I just met. This was just…one of those things. So I wasn't expecting any more than one night."

"Neither was I."

She stole a glance at Bullet. Or rather Clay. They hadn't actually lied to each other. They'd just withheld information that would have helped them avoid doing something like this.

"Are Poncho and Duck in the military, too?" she asked.

"No, they're actually civilians visiting me. And I took a week off to stay with them. I didn't mean to trick you…"

At this point, she figured it didn't matter. But for some reason, it did. "I wasn't trying to pull the wool over your eyes, either. I flew in from Houston last night and don't have to sign in until tomorrow night. I didn't see any point in sharing my life story."

Although, to be honest, she wished they still had one more day together. But it wouldn't be right.

"Well," he said, nodding toward the door. "I'd better get out of here. Otherwise, I'd be tempted to climb back into bed."

She smiled, clinging to the admission like a compliment.

"I wish things were different," he added.

So did she. Their chemistry was off the charts. At least in bed. And before reality struck, she'd been ruing the thought of going back to her barracks and him flying back to Texas. But this was different. Worse.

So close, yet so far away.

She managed an unaffected smile. "I guess I'll see you around."

He stood in the center of the room for a couple of beats, as if he was struggling with reality and ethics and everything else. "Take care."

"You, too." Rickie watched him walk toward the door.

While it was possible they'd run into each other again, she hoped not. It would be awkward at best. Not to mention disappointing.

But an officer fraternizing with an enlisted soldier

was against Army regulations, and since she wasn't about to make any changes to her career plan, their short-term affair was officially over. Wham, bam, thank you…sir.

Chapter Three

After Bullet—or rather, Captain Masters—walked out the door and told her he was returning to the beach house he and his friends had rented, Rickie felt an unexpected loss. She realized the best game plan and her only option was to avoid him like a bad case of mono sweeping through the barracks. So without waiting for the sun to rise, she packed her bags and checked out of the bungalow a day early.

When she reached her car, a twelve-year-old Honda she'd purchased when she first arrived on the island, she took one last look at the darkened beach house where Clay was staying. She didn't see any lights on inside. Apparently, she was the only one who'd lost sleep over their lovemaking, and that only served to make her feel worse and more determined to escape.

Yet even though leaving now meant she could avoid Clay while here on the North Shore, there was a real possibility that she'd run into him in the future.

Which was why, when she got back to Schofield Barracks, she began to constantly scan her surroundings whenever she went to the PX or any other place where she might see him and tried to mentally prepare for an awkward meeting.

Oddly enough, when she didn't spot him, she'd go back to her car feeling both glad and disappointed.

While Rickie worked at the clinic each day, a steady flow of soldiers came in, each one presenting different ailments and injuries that kept her busy, and she began to think she might have put it all behind her. That was, until she finally spotted Clay two weeks later.

She was in her car, preparing to cross the street from Schofield Barracks to Wheeler Airfield, where the clinic was located. While waiting for the traffic light to turn green, she noticed him up ahead, standing near the curb and talking to several other uniformed soldiers. They all bore a similarity, but she recognized Clay instantly. There was something about him, a mesmerizing swagger, that made him stand out in a crowd.

The moment he looked up and zeroed in on her car, her breath caught, her heartbeat stalled.

He turned away from the men and studied her so intently that she realized he hadn't put that night behind him, either.

But so what? There wasn't anything either of them could do about it now. So she gripped the steering wheel tight until the light turned green. As she drove past him, she gave a slight nod and continued on her way.

Three days later, while parking in front of the clinic to start her shift, she caught sight of him again. He was jogging along the street wearing a black T-shirt, Army-issue shorts and running shoes. Apparently, he was finishing his morning PT. She expected him to keep running, but he surprised her by turning off the path he'd been following and crossing the street to approach her car.

With his light brown hair mussed and damp with perspiration, he was a vision to behold. He'd shaved this morning, which revealed a professional side to him. A military side.

She reminded herself of his rank, of the serious consequences they'd face if their one night together turned into a second and a third. The first time they'd made love had been a mistake, a misunderstanding. But there was no way they could continue to see each other.

Yet she couldn't keep her eyes off his sweat-dampened T-shirt, which clung to his muscular chest and his taut abs. As he closed the short distance between them, her pulse thundered, matching the cadence of his steps, and when he slowed to a stop, her heart rate darn near skidded to a complete halt.

"Hey," he said. "How's it going?"

"Fine." She managed to tear her gaze away from his body, but she couldn't seem to get her pulse under control. "I'm doing okay. How 'bout you?"

"I can't complain." He nodded toward the clinic entrance. "So you work here, huh?"

"Yes, I do. And I assume you live nearby."

"Yep, just a couple streets away." He glanced to his right, and then to the left, as if checking for eavesdroppers prone to gossip or tattle. When they both realized the coast was clear, he said, "I wish things could be different."

He'd made that same comment after they'd made love and realized they'd have to go their own ways. And she'd replayed his words a hundred times over the past couple of weeks, convincing herself that he'd meant everything he'd ever told her that night. "I wish things could have played out differently, too, but that's just the way it is."

He nodded his agreement, yet rather than end the conversation and go about his business, he continued to stand there, hesitant. Gorgeous. And temporarily stripped of rank in those running shorts.

"Have you already reenlisted?" he asked.

His question struck her as odd. Was he wondering if she'd decided to opt out of the military? Was he reminding her in a roundabout way that she could change her mind?

If she did, they could continue to date. Was that what he was getting at? Maybe, but she wouldn't take that risk. The Army was her family, and if she gave it all up, hoping that something might actually come of an affair with a man she barely knew, she'd end up in worse shape than she was now. At least, emotionally.

She'd learned early on—and the hard way—that the people she cared about didn't stick around very long, so civilian life wasn't an option.

"No, I haven't reupped yet, but I plan to do it soon. They're going to give me a signing bonus." She nodded toward the Honda that had seen better days. "Then I'll be able to buy a new car."

"Good for you."

She thought so, too. Yet for some reason, as she continued to study Clay, as she remembered lying in his arms, she didn't feel all that lucky. But she couldn't let that sway her. There were more important things in life than momentary pleasure.

"I like being in the Army," she added. "And I love my job."

"That's good. Apparently, you made a wise career choice when you enlisted. Being a medic is obviously a good fit."

He was right. She'd scored at the top of her class while in school at AIT. And she'd been told many times that she was a top-notch medic. She thrived on being needed. And she appreciated the praise from Captain Nguyen, her commanding officer.

"I've wanted to work in the medical field for almost as long as I can remember," she said. "In fact, I'm going to get a nursing degree one of these days."

"That's admirable. I had a childhood dream to become a soldier, like my dad."

She smiled. "Mine started when I was a kid, too. My twin sister, Lainie, suffered from several medical problems when we were little, and I used to look after her the best I could."

"You have a twin?"

"I used to. She died when we were nine."

He frowned, compassion filling his eyes. "I'm sorry."

"Thanks." She sighed. "It was tough. She passed away during open-heart surgery. And it was about that time that I decided to be a nurse or a doctor. I wanted to do something to help people who were sick and injured."

"So why did you decide to join the military?" Clay asked. "You could have gone to nursing school as a civilian."

Again his questioning took her aback. And now it was her turn to look to the left, and then to the right, checking for eavesdroppers.

There was no one around, thank goodness. But even if there were, so what? They were just having an innocent conversation.

"I took a health class in high school, which was really interesting, and that locked in my decision to have a career in the medical field. I didn't want to take out any student loans, so I decided to join the military. My father was a retired ensign in the Navy, and he hoped that I would follow in his footsteps. But I chose the Army instead, became a medic and ended up stationed here."

He nodded sagely, as if that answered all the questions he had about her and about…their situation.

"Well," he said, as he glanced toward the street and the path on which he'd been running, "I guess I'd better let you get to work."

He was giving her an out, an excuse to end their conversation. And she really ought to take it, but it still left her a little uneasy, not to mention disappointed. She'd never feel Bullet's hands caress her again.

No, *not* Bullet. *Captain Masters*. She wasn't even supposed to call him Clay.

"I'll see you around," he said.

She supposed that was a given. And their future run-ins were sure to be uncomfortable, but there wasn't much either of them could do about that now. So she offered him what she hoped was a casual smile. "Take care."

"Will do." Then he turned and jogged away, leaving her to stare after him and rue all that might have been if their circumstances had only been different.

As Clay ran along the side of the road, he had a growing compulsion to look over his shoulder and catch one last glimpse of Rickie, but he forced himself to focus on the path ahead. He'd known that they'd probably see each other again, and sure enough, they had.

He could have ignored her and pretended that they'd never met, but he wouldn't do that. He might avoid making commitments, but he wasn't a jerk. He was respectful to his ex-lovers.

And what a lover she'd been. She had a fiery passion that had turned him inside out, and he doubted he'd experience anything like that again. He'd never been one to rate the women he'd dated, but she'd get a gold star.

She looked a lot different this morning than she had the day he'd met her, when she'd been wearing that sexy red bikini. And later that evening, when she'd been naked, lying next to him in bed.

Of course, now that they'd been intimate, he'd find her just as beautiful dressed in battle fatigues and combat boots. He had a feeling that, each time he saw her, he was going to be tempted to do more than greet her and have a friendly little chat.

And that was the problem. In the past, he'd never had any trouble moving on when a fling was coming to an end. He'd always been able to keep his hormones in check. But he wasn't having an easy time of it now. For some weird reason, he couldn't seem to shake off his thoughts of Rickie.

There seemed to be something different about her, something that drew him to her and made him want to challenge military protocol when it came to fraternization.

He wouldn't cross any lines, though, even if he still had a dormant rebellious streak. When he'd been a foot-loose kid in Texas, it used to flare sky-high. He'd also thrived on the adrenaline rush—much to the chagrin of his mother, who'd been determined to keep him safe.

The poor woman had really flipped out when she learned he'd been accepted for admission at West Point. But what had she expected from a kid who'd grown up idolizing his late father, a decorated war hero who was still held in the highest esteem by everyone back home?

You'd think she would've been proud that Clay had decided to become an Army officer, but she'd cried for days, sure he'd be sent off to war and would die in battle, like his father had.

He'd told her that he understood her worries, but he felt a strong conviction to serve.

"There are lots of ways you can help people. You could be a doctor or a fireman or a teacher."

"Most mothers would be proud that their kid was accepted at West Point."

"I am, honey, but why couldn't you have gone to Texas A&M?" she'd asked. "That way, you would have been close to home. Then, after graduating with some kind of an agriculture degree, you could have helped your granddad and me on the ranch."

But Clay had never wanted to be a rancher.

Even his wild, fun-loving friends had followed his lead and turned onto a straight and narrow path. Duck was now a champion bronc rider, determined to help the Rocking Chair Rodeo promote a ranch for retired cowboys, as well as Kidville, a nearby group home for kids. And Poncho had become a cop who did his best to keep the town of Wexler safe.

Of course, considering the jobs the three buddies now had, they were still hooked on the rush when faced with danger or the unknown.

With each stride Clay took, running away from the clinic where Rickie worked, voices from the past hounded him.

Rules were meant to be broken.

When he reached the corner, about fifty yards from the clinic, he jogged in place and waited for the light to turn green. But within a couple of beats, the compulsion to look at Rickie became too strong to ignore.

He glanced over his shoulder, but she was no longer standing outside. Then again, he really hadn't expected her to be. By now, she had to be inside working. Out of sight.

Untouchable.

Off-limits.

Yet memories of their amazing night together hit him hard once more, and temptation stirred his blood. He'd give just about anything to make love with her again. But he wouldn't cross the line.

He might have been a rebel while growing up, but he played by the rules now. He had to, no matter how badly he wanted to see Rickie again.

There was also something more than military regulations holding him back, preventing him from doing something stupid that would screw up his career.

Sergeant Erica Campbell was a professional. A medic and a dedicated soldier. She loved her job, too. And she'd made it clear that she had no intention of giving it up.

And neither would he.

For the next few weeks, Rickie went about her usual duties, which kept her mind busy during the day. Nights, however, were a different story.

She'd lost count of the number of times she'd dreamed about a romantic evening on the beach, slow dancing with a handsome cowboy, resting her cheek against his broad, muscular chest, hearing the gentle thumps of his heart and relishing his charming Texas drawl.

Then she'd wake up to reality.

She had no business dreaming about Captain Clay Masters now, let alone sleeping with him back then. Sure, it had been an easy mistake to make and one that was explainable, if they were ever questioned about it.

Intellectually, she knew that. But tell that to the memory that continued to batter her heart.

She'd never believed in love at first sight, but it seemed as if she'd experienced more than a memorable orgasm that night. Apparently, there'd been an emotional connection, too. If not, then why would that evening continue to play out in her mind whether she was awake or asleep?

Heck, here she was, wrapping up the last hour of her shift at the clinic and daydreaming about the guy again. She couldn't seem to catch a break.

As she passed by the supply cabinet, her commanding officer called out, "Erica? Can you give me a hand?"

Rickie turned to Captain Veronica Nguyen, a petite brunette who was a physician's assistant—and probably the best the military had to offer. Not only was she a sharp diagnostician, but she had a great bedside manner.

"What's up?" Rickie asked.

"I have to suture a patient, and the injury is a bit complex. Will you assist?"

"Of course." Rickie appreciated having the distraction.

As they walked toward one of the exam rooms, the captain slowed her steps and pointed to the bulletin board that hung on the wall. "Oh, that reminds me. I'm taking leave on Friday. My grandmother is in the hospital and isn't doing well, so I'm going to fly back to the mainland to visit her and to check on her myself."

"That's too bad," Rickie said. "I hope it's not serious."

"Me, too." The captain pointed to the calendar. "Yesterday afternoon, I marked off the days that I'll be gone, but I didn't get a chance to tell you. Captain Schwartz is going to cover for me."

"No problem. I'm sure we'll be okay." Rickie glanced at the red line that stretched through the following week, and a troubling thought crossed her mind.

She counted backward to the day she'd met Clay on the North Shore and then to her last period.

Uh-oh. She was late. And she'd always been regular. Could she be…?

No, that wasn't possible. They'd used protection that night.

Of course, things had been pretty heated. They might have gotten a little reckless while caught up in passion. Also she'd had that condom for a long time. Had she kept it past the expiration date?

Cut it out, Rickie. You're letting your imagination take flight.

There had to be another reason for skipping a period. Nerves and stress could do a real number on a person's health and their hormones. This was probably just a fluke. Or a miscalculation of some kind. That would explain it.

Yet she couldn't deny that it was possible. She could be pregnant. And if she was, having a baby was going to be a real game changer in terms of her future plans and goals.

Oddly enough, as unsettling as that reality might be, a quiver of excitement built. If she were to have a child, a son or daughter to love and care for, she'd have a family again.

In time, she might have handled the losses fate had

dealt her fairly well, but she'd been devastated when Lainie died, and to this day it felt as if a large part of her heart and soul was missing.

Maybe that's what was going on. Rickie wanted to be part of a family so badly that her psyche was playing a trick on her and her body was going along with it. She wasn't pregnant. She just wanted to be so she could have someone to love.

But there would be plenty of time to have a baby in the future—when she was married and had a house to bring her little one home to.

So she shook off the stray thought and hurried to the exam room to assist Captain Nguyen. She even managed to get through the last hour of her day without dwelling on the possibility that she and Clay had conceived a baby.

That was, until she walked out to her car and spotted him again. He was wearing a flight suit and headed toward one of the hangars. She expected him to continue on his way, but when their eyes met, her heart flip-flopped. And when he crossed the street and walked toward her, her heart rumbled in her chest.

"How's it going?" he asked, that slight Texas twang a calming caress, soothing her like his hands once had.

Funny you should ask, she was tempted to say. *My period is late, and I might be…*

Again, she shook off the possibility, as well as the urge to even bring up the topic. "I'm fine. Same old, same old."

She glanced at his uniform—the flight suit he wore

so well. Her gaze traveled up to his face, to those dazzling green eyes.

If they were to have a baby, would its eyes…?

Oh, for Pete's sake, Rickie. Stop it.

"Are you heading out or coming in?" she asked.

"Going out. Night training on the Big Island."

She nodded, wondering which medic would be joining his squadron and wishing it was her. Not tonight, of course. But…maybe someday.

"I'd like to talk to you," he said.

"About…?"

He scanned their surroundings, then lowered his voice to a near whisper. "About that night."

Under normal circumstances, she might have told him that wasn't a good idea to broach the subject. Wouldn't it be best if they forgot it all together?

Yeah, right. If there'd been any way she could do that, she would have done it already. And if her period didn't show up soon, she'd have something to talk to him about, too.

"All right," she said. "Maybe some time next week?"

He nodded his agreement. "We could meet in Waikiki."

She was tempted to suggest someplace on the North Shore, but that was a bad idea. And one that was wrong.

"Have you gotten that bonus?" he asked.

"I haven't reupped yet." And if she actually was pregnant, she'd have to rethink that decision. She'd be a single mother, and if she were deployed, she wouldn't have anyone to take care of the baby. Talk about unexpected surprises.

As if he could read her mind, Clay blessed her with a charming grin.

What was that about? Did he sense she was facing a dilemma of some kind? Did he think she would reconsider an Army career so she'd be free to date him?

As contrary as that might be to her career goal, a small, girlish side of her hoped that's what he meant.

"Hey, Masters," another soldier called out from a nearby hangar.

Clay turned to him. "What's up?"

"Major Ramos is looking for you."

Clay nodded toward the hangar. "I'd better go. I'll see you later."

"All right." In the meantime, she'd have to find out if she really was expecting a baby.

It would be easy enough to have a test at the clinic, but she didn't want anyone to know her secret. Not yet. So she'd have to purchase a kit that she could use in the privacy of her bathroom.

If the test turned out positive, she'd have to tell Clay. Wouldn't she?

A child deserved to know its father, especially if he was an upright, admirable man. A leader. A protector.

She took one last look at the Black Hawk commander who was striding toward a nearby hangar. They might have thought their sexual encounter was a onetime thing, but the result of it could be a lot more lasting than that. Especially if they were going to be parents.

But first things first. She'd have to find out for sure.

And if the test results were negative, she could get her mind back on an even keel.

And off the man who'd occupied her dreams ever since the night they'd met.

Chapter Four

The next morning, right after Rickie entered the clinic, Captain Nguyen met her near the supply room. Her dark hair was pulled into a tight military bun, and she was dressed in uniform, but the expression she wore was more serious than usual.

"Is something wrong?" Rickie asked.

"Not here at the clinic. It's just that…" She slowly shook her head and sighed. "I hate bad news."

Had the captain's grandmother taken a turn for the worse? Had she passed away during the night? Rickie didn't want to pry, so she awaited the explanation she hoped was coming.

"There was a flight mishap on the Big Island last night," Captain Nguyen said. "A Black Hawk went down at the Pohakuloa Training Area."

Rickie's heart dropped to the pit of her stomach. Clay had gone out on a night training. Had he been involved?

Maybe not. But he certainly would know the soldiers who were. He also might have been part of the rescue operation, which would have been tough.

Still, he could have been injured, although she prayed he wasn't. Yet fear continued to build until she couldn't keep quiet any longer.

"Was…" She cleared her throat, trying to dislodge the worry and any sign of emotional involvement. "Was anyone injured?"

"Unfortunately, yes. One of the squadron commanders got the worst of it, although he'll pull through."

An overwhelming sense of dread hung over her like rain-drenched cammies, weighing her down and chilling her to the bone. Her pulse thundered in her ears and a tsunami of curiosity flooded her thoughts.

She had a slew of questions to fire at the captain, but she bit her tongue, knowing she had to remain professional. And removed from any personal involvement.

Finally, she asked, "Do you know who was injured?"

"Captain Masters and Sergeant Clemmons, the crew chief. They were treated at the scene, then airlifted to Tripler."

Panic struck hard, balling up in Rickie's throat, making it hard to breathe, let alone speak. But then again, Captain Nguyen had said the injuries weren't life threatening, which was a relief.

"How badly was he—or rather, *they*—hurt?" Rickie asked.

Captain Nguyen eyed her intently—maybe even suspiciously. She didn't say a word, but her expression seemed to ask, *Why the special interest?*

Rickie wasn't about to admit that she'd had a one-night fling with the Black Hawk commander—albeit after a case of mistaken identity. And even though they'd agreed to go their own ways, she felt a connection to him, one that might now include a baby.

But the complexity of her weird feelings was hard enough for her to understand, let alone to put into words that would make sense. Either way, she regretted that she hadn't picked up a home pregnancy test yesterday. No matter how complicated a positive result might be, she needed to know for sure.

"It's always tough to hear about serious training injuries and flight mishaps," Captain Nguyen said. "But let's try to put it behind us. We have a full schedule today."

Rickie nodded, hoping she could do just that. But the CO had implied those injuries were serious, even if they weren't life threatening. So once her shift at the clinic ended, she was going to drive out to Tripler Army Medical Center in Honolulu and check on Clay's condition herself. Surely a hospital visit wouldn't be considered fraternization.

But right now, she didn't care if it was.

Clay had drifted in and out of consciousness all day, thanks to what the attending medic had called head trauma and the pain meds he'd been given. His leg hurt like hell and was in traction. One of his eyes was bandaged, and his vision in the other was blurred. He assumed he'd gotten a serious concussion, because his thoughts were scrambled and he wasn't entirely sure what had happened.

Now, as a physician stood at his bedside, explaining the extent of his injuries, he tried his best to focus.

"You did a real number on your knee, but it'll heal and, given time and physical therapy, you shouldn't have trouble walking. But I'm afraid that leg may never be at one hundred percent. You also have a head injury that damaged your optic nerve. You may not lose your vision in that eye, but it's likely to be impaired. That all being said, it looks like you won't be fit for duty. So you'll be getting a medical discharge."

Clay's brain had been scrambled. Maybe he hadn't heard that right. "Excuse me?"

"You're not going to be fit for duty, son. As far as the military is concerned, it's case closed. But on the bright side, you'll be able to do most of the things you're used to doing."

"Can I fly again?" he asked.

"With a vision defect, it's doubtful."

Clay closed his good eye as disappointment swirled like a Texas twister, wreaking havoc in his disjointed thoughts. Maybe he'd wake up and this would be a bad dream. A hallucination triggered by pain pills.

"Do you have any questions?" the doctor asked.

"Yeah. Are you sure about that discharge?"

The doctor nodded. "I'm afraid so, son. The military puts the needs of the aircraft and the crew above those of the individual. You must be operationally ready and fit for duty at all times."

Clay turned to him, his good eye attempting to focus on the shadowy figure before him. "You don't know me, Doc. I heal quickly. And I'll work harder than anyone else. I'll be back at one hundred percent before you know it."

"The ultimate decision is out of my hands. It's up to the MEB and the PEB."

The medical and physical evaluations boards. A bunch of upper-level doctors who decided who got to stay and who had to be medically discharged. Was this really happening?

"I'm sorry to be giving you bad news," the doctor said.

It wasn't just bad. It was devastating. Sure, Clay would recover. And he'd walk again. He could handle the pain and the extensive rehab he was facing. He was tough and determined to heal. But none of that seemed to matter when his military career was over.

The head injury, a serious concussion, was no big deal. He'd had one when he'd crashed his bike and another when he'd played football in high school. He'd suffered a multiple fracture in his leg. He could deal with that, too. But the fatal blow, the parting shot, was the damage to his eye, the effect it would have on his vision. And that meant he couldn't fly.

Everything he loved—the Army, piloting Black Hawks, commanding a squadron—was being taken away from him. And the reality sent his hope plummeting.

What in the hell did he have left?

Talk about tailspins. His entire identity lay in his military service. If not a soldier and a pilot, who was he?

A rancher? A *farmer*?

He closed his good eye once more and blew out a ragged sigh.

"You were lucky," Dr. Simmons said.

Clay didn't feel the least bit lucky. His injuries hadn't killed him, which should make him happy. But they'd put a complete halt to his military career. Hell, even if he wanted to work as a crop duster—and he damn sure didn't—he wouldn't be able to.

He tried his best to look on the bright side. He was going home to Texas, where he still had friends and family. But that didn't lift his mood in the least.

Life as he knew it, as he'd always dreamed it would be, was over. And as far as he was concerned, nothing was going to make him feel better.

It seemed like forever before Rickie was able to leave the clinic and drive to Tripler, a huge coral-pink structure located on the slopes of Moanalua Ridge. If Clay had to be treated anywhere, this was the place. Tripler was the largest military hospital serving the Asian and Pacific Rims.

On the drive down the H-1 to the H-201, she gripped the steering wheel with clammy hands. By the time she parked, entered the hospital and learned where his room was located, her heart was pounding like thundering luau drums, and her legs felt as immobile as tree stumps. But she managed to follow the directions she'd been given.

She paused in the doorway and spotted the bed where a single male patient lay. She'd been told his injuries weren't life threatening, but they had to hurt like hell. His head was bandaged, one eye was covered in gauze and his right leg was in traction.

Her first impulse was to hurry to his bedside to soothe him, to caress his face and whisper words of comfort. She'd always been a nurturer. But then again, maybe in this case, she merely wanted to be near the man with whom she'd once been intimate.

Either way, she held her emotions in check and entered slowly, her boot steps making far more noise than she'd like.

"Hey," she said, gentling her voice as if she were approaching a stray dog with a wounded paw.

Clay turned to the door, and when he spotted her, recognition dawned in the eye that wasn't bandaged, but he didn't even offer the hint of a smile. "You shouldn't be here."

He was right, but checking in on him had been a growing compulsion she hadn't been able to squelch. "I heard you were going to be hospitalized for a while, and since I was in the neighborhood, I thought I'd stop by to see you."

He didn't respond, but she approached his bed anyway. "Captain Nguyen told me about the flight mishap. I was sorry to hear about it."

"Not as sorry as me." He turned his head away and glanced out the window.

Had it been his fault? Was he assuming responsibility for the downed helicopter? Did he feel as if he'd caused his crew chief's injury?

"Those things happen," she said.

"Not to me."

Okay, then. She'd dealt with surly patients before. In this case, she figured it was the pain he was in, the medication they'd given him.

"I could sneak you in some better food," she said. "Maybe a big juicy cheeseburger with all the fixings. Some chocolate cake…"

He slowly shook his head.

"You shouldn't be here," he said again.

She knew that. But she'd come anyway. She hadn't been able to stay away, although his tone and his obvious discomfort with her presence caused her to regret the impulse to visit.

Yet she'd wanted to see him, to learn the extent of his injuries for herself. And she wasn't about to ponder why. She damn well knew why she was here. Something had stirred inside her that night they'd met. And right now, it was possible that a little someone was stirring in her womb. A child they'd created.

But she didn't dare voice a possibility like that. Not here. Not now.

"How's your crew chief?" she asked.

"He'll live. And he'll fly again." Something in his harsh tone, his lack of sympathy for the guy, suggested there was more to it than that.

But she knew better than to press for information he wasn't yet willing to give. So she said, "That's good."

"Yeah. For him."

Her stomach knotted, forming something cold and hard that dropped to her gut. "But not for you?"

He turned back to face her. "No. I'm going to end

up with a medical discharge." He lifted a bruised hand to his bandaged eye. "And I'll most likely have a vision problem that means I'll never fly again."

"I'm sorry."

He let out a guttural sound, something raw and torn that revealed a wound deep inside, one that couldn't be seen or treated with gauze or pain medication.

She hurt for him, grieved deep in her heart. She knew the Army was his life, as it was hers. Yet, on the other hand, if he was getting out, that took the fraternization issue off the table.

"Well, I can come back to visit you, and when you're released we could keep seeing each other." She hesitated, realizing this was a fresh wound for him in more ways than one. "I mean, technically we're not crossing any forbidden lines anymore, so—"

He slowly shook his head. "Don't bother. I'll be going back to Texas as soon as I'm discharged."

Now, there was a downside she hadn't considered.

He cleared his throat. "Listen, Sergeant, I'm not feeling very good. I need to get some rest."

She could certainly understand that, but the fact that he'd called her by her rank rather than her name said a lot more than his actual words. And so did his tone. She tried to blame it on his obvious disappointment at his diagnosis, on the pain and his medication. Yet it still hurt to be dismissed.

"Sure, I'll let you get some rest. But I'll be back." She'd have to, especially if that pregnancy test revealed what she feared it might.

"Like I said, *don't*."

She nodded, then turned and walked away, accepting the news like a good soldier. But before she got two steps down the hospital corridor, tears filled her eyes and an ache settled deep in her heart.

Clay wasn't the only one whose plans had gone awry. She was facing her own dilemma. And apparently, he wasn't going to be much help to her.

Not only did Clay hurt like hell, he felt like an ass. He hadn't meant to treat Rickie that way, to be so rude, but he'd just suffered a devastating blow. He'd hardly had ten minutes to digest the doctor's diagnosis, which had been far more crippling than a bum leg or vision problems, when she'd popped up unexpectedly.

Just the sight of her had made things all the worse. Sure, he was tempted to reach out to her, to accept her concern and sympathy. But that would have only complicated the issue.

Guilt continued to niggle at him, building until it rose up and struck him like a football helmet to the chest. He glanced at the empty doorway, where she'd once stood.

He'd more or less dismissed her like a bumbling new recruit. But he couldn't deal with that now. Not when he was still struggling to wrap his mind around his new reality.

Granted, he could use a little comfort and TLC right now. But not the kind Rickie would bring. She seemed to think that, once he was discharged from the Army, they could continue seeing each other, which would never work.

Even if he were up for a relationship of some kind,

he'd be damned if he'd sit back as a civilian and watch her Army career take off. Not when his had just crashed and burned.

Besides, he wasn't the kind of guy who'd settle down with one woman. A commitment like that usually led to marriage, and Clay refused to even contemplate being tied down with anyone, even Rickie.

He'd only been five when his father had deployed for Desert Storm, and he'd been six when they'd gotten word his dad had died in battle. So he'd been too young to remember or to pay any attention to his parents' interactions. His stepgrandmother and Granddad had split up right before Clay and his mom had moved to the Bar M, so they hadn't set any long-term romantic examples, either.

Poncho had grown up in foster care, and Duck had been raised by his uncle, a single cowboy who'd sworn off women after his fiancée ran off with a country-western singer bound for Nashville. And some of Clay's military friends, the few guys who were married, didn't seem to be all that happy. Maybe it had to do with added responsibilities and curfews. After all, he'd heard that old saying—happy wife, happy life.

As far as Clay was concerned, a wife or even a serious girlfriend would clip his wings—if that blasted flight mishap hadn't already torn them off.

So he wouldn't consider a relationship with Rickie. Even if she decided not to reenlist and moved back to Texas, it wouldn't work. They lived in different cities located at least fifty miles apart. Maybe more than that.

No, it was best that Clay had pretty much ended what

little thing they might have had and run her off. She'd be happier that way. And so would he. In a few weeks, he'd be back home, waiting for his head to clear and his bones to mend. Then he'd work the family spread, taking some of the responsibility off his mom and Granddad. Even if he'd had other options, it was only right that he step up and take his turn.

Still, he'd never wanted to be a rancher or a cowboy. Not day in and day out, season after season. It'd make for a boring life, if you asked him. Yet now it was the only viable option he had, and he rolled his eyes at his new normal.

Yippee ki-yay.

After leaving Tripler, Rickie stopped by a pharmacy and purchased an over-the-counter pregnancy test. But instead of taking it home, she pulled into a nearby fast food restaurant and parked. She wasn't hungry, even though she'd had a light lunch and it was already past her usual dinner hour.

She was too nervous to eat, but since she wanted an excuse for going inside to use the restroom, she ordered a cheeseburger to go. While it was being prepared, she carried her small shopping bag into the ladies' room.

In the privacy of a stall, she opened the package. While holding the testing apparatus in one hand, she read the instructions. It was all pretty simple. If she was pregnant, a plus sign would form. If not, she'd see a minus. It wouldn't take long.

So she followed the directions and waited for the results. She was both excited and frightened at the prospect of being pregnant, which made no sense. She ought to be scared spitless after the way Clay had treated her, after the words he'd said. He'd made it clear that she'd be facing parenthood on her own.

She'd held her head high as she left his hospital room, but it hadn't been easy not to crumple at the way he'd treated her. It wasn't just his words and tone that had hurt her. He'd brushed off that night they'd shared on the North Shore like a stale bread crumb, when she'd considered it special. Apparently, their lovemaking meant nothing to him, which only served to gradually turn her hurt to anger.

She glanced at the test, afraid to look yet afraid not to. Talk about being mixed up and confused.

As a plus sign began as a light shade of baby blue and then darkened, she slowly shook her head. She was pregnant. With Clay's baby.

Now what?

She was both shaken and delighted—shaken because she didn't have any experience with babies, and now she was going to be a single mom. Yet at the same time, she was happy to know she was going to have someone to love, someone to love her back.

At this point, she had no idea if that little someone would be a girl or a boy. That really didn't matter.

But something else did. That son or daughter was going to need her. So how could she consider staying in the military and facing potential deployments? She didn't have any family support, so she wouldn't have anyone to keep her baby for her while she was gone, even if it was just for a weekend training. And if truth be told, even if she did find a trusted sitter, she wasn't going to leave her child in someone else's care.

She would raise her child on her own. It would be better that way. She just had to put some thought into the future and make a game plan. It would be difficult, but not impossible.

Besides, she had a lot more going for her than many single mothers did. She even had a mortgage-free home in Jeffersville. That is, if the busy handyman she'd lined up had actually found time to complete the repairs and paint the place.

The more she thought about moving back to Texas, putting her own mark on that little brick house and making it a home for herself and her baby, the more she liked the idea. It was the perfect solution.

As she tossed away the used testing apparatus, she thought of something else. She'd be living an hour or so away from Clay's hometown of Wexler. Not that it mattered, but she'd have to tell him about the baby. He might even want to...

No, he wouldn't. But he did deserve to know he was going to be a father, didn't he?

She'd have to tell him, even if it complicated his life. It might complicate hers, too.

Could she handle seeing Clay for visitations, birthday parties and school events? Would the sight of him always remind her of how that sweet baby was placed in her womb?

Surely, she'd get used to seeing him, to figuring out a way to coparent. Besides, the baby deserved to know its daddy.

There might also be a concern about genetics, family illnesses and that sort of thing.

By the time she returned to the barracks, her appetite had returned, and she'd wolfed down the cheeseburger. She'd also created a solid game plan.

She wasn't going to reenlist. Instead, she'd go home to Texas and fix up a nursery in her old bedroom. She'd also use her GI Bill benefits to pay for nursing school. In the meantime, she'd apply for a job at one of the hospitals. There was no telling when a suitable position would open up, but at least she could get her name in the system. She'd also have to find a competent and loving nanny, but she had about seven months to do that.

How hard could it be?

Chapter Five

It had been three months since the flight mishap ended Clay's military career, and he was finally back on the Bar M, trying to settle into life as a cattleman.

His knee was on the mend, although it was still giving him trouble and he had to rely on a cane whenever he walked on uneven ground. But it was coming along okay, thanks to the physical therapy department at the Brighton Valley Medical Center and Clay's determination to push through the pain.

It sucked to work so hard to be whole again, but how many times had he told his men "Embrace the suck"?

His head injury had healed, and he could see well enough. But his vision still wasn't as good as it had been. He supposed that was to be expected after the optic nerve damage. At least he wasn't blind in one eye.

In some ways, it was good to be home. Duck and Poncho stopped by regularly and did their best to cheer him up. It worked, but only while they were visiting. After that, reality set in, and he had to face the fact that he'd given up an exciting life for one that was so-so at best.

His mom and grandfather were happy to have him back on the Bar M, and while he tried to accept the fact that his life had changed, he couldn't seem to escape the dark mood that followed him after his hospital stay at Tripler.

He tried to shake it by spending most of his waking hours outdoors in the sunshine, but he still couldn't do much work yet, at least not the heavy stuff that would ease Granddad's daily load. So most of the time he sat on the front porch, just like he was doing this afternoon.

The screen door squeaked open, and his mom stepped outside. "Can I bring you something to drink? Lemonade or maybe some sweet tea?"

"No, thanks. I'm okay for now."

She continued to stand there, as if he might change his mind. She did that a lot these days, waiting on him and hanging around as if she might be able to say or do something that would set things back to right and lift his mood once and for all.

But she couldn't help. Like the physical therapist told him again today, some things just take time.

"There's some leftover German chocolate cake," she added. "I'd be happy to bring you a slice."

Clay appreciated her attempts to make things better, and while she tried her damnedest, that was something he'd have to do on his own, and so far, he hadn't had much luck.

On the other hand, she made no secret of the fact that she was pleased to have him home—safe and sound— even if he wasn't the happy-go-lucky son she'd once had.

Clay understood that. He really did. But what she believed was a blessing and a wonderful turn of events he considered bad luck.

"I worry about you," she said, moving in closer. "You've lost weight, and you're not eating like you should. I wish you'd at least take those vitamins I got you."

"I'm fine." He stroked his bum knee, hoping to ease the ache without resorting to another dose of extra-strength ibuprofen tablets. "The doctors and my physical therapist haven't complained."

She lifted her hand to shield her eyes from the glare of the afternoon sun. The quick action reminded him of a half-ass salute and of the life he'd been forced to give up.

"All right," she said. "Then I'll try not to worry. But it's not easy being a mom."

Motherhood had never been easy for her. She still tended to hover over him, much like she did when he was a kid. He'd resented it then, enough to rebel every chance he got. And it still bothered him now— especially since he was no longer a rebellious adolescent, who could escape by sneaking out his bedroom window to meet his friends. About the only escape he got these days was the drive back and forth to the medical center for physical therapy.

His mom stepped around his bad leg, which he'd stretched out in front of him, and sat beside him. Before she could change the subject, an unfamiliar car drove into the yard.

"Looks like we have company," she said, getting to her feet. "Or else someone took a wrong turn and needs directions. I'll check on it."

Clay didn't give the vehicle a second thought until the driver's door opened and he spotted the pretty brunette getting out.

What was Rickie doing here? Had she gotten transferred to a base in Texas?

She'd traded in her Army uniform for a pair of black jeans and a pink blouse. Her hair shimmered in the afternoon sun, the curls tumbling over her shoulders. She'd always caused him to sit up and take notice, and today was no different.

He studied her as she approached the porch. She looked…different. He couldn't put his finger on it. There was a new look in her eye; a glow that had nothing to do with the afternoon sunshine. And while her curves had attracted him on the beach, she looked even sexier now. He had to admit that he was not only surprised to see her but actually glad she'd come.

"Hey," she said, as she reached the first step to the wraparound porch.

"What a surprise." Clay probably ought to stand and greet her, which was the polite thing to do, but he'd just gotten home from physical therapy, and his knee hurt like hell.

His mom, on the other hand, took up the slack on

courtesy, because she quickly greeted Rickie with an outstretched hand. "I take it you're one of Clay's friends. I'm his mother, Sandra. It's nice to meet you."

"I'm Erica Campbell. But you can call me Rickie."

Mom turned to Clay, her expression quizzical and begging for details. When he'd been a kid, that look had bothered him, so he would clam up to protect his privacy. And, admittedly, to piss her off. But he couldn't really blame her for being curious today. He hadn't expected to see Rickie again, and he wondered why she'd come.

"Rickie and I met in Hawaii," Clay explained. "We were both stationed there."

His mother brightened and blessed Rickie with a warm and welcoming smile. "I'm glad you dropped by. Can I get you something to drink? I have fresh-squeezed lemonade. And I always have a pitcher of sweet tea on the counter."

"Sure," Rickie said. "I'll have whatever is easiest. Thanks."

As soon as his mother hurried into the house, leaving them alone, Rickie made her approach. "I hope you don't mind me stopping by."

"Not at all. It's been a long time. How'd you find this place?"

"It wasn't hard. I did an internet search, then used my GPS system."

He glanced at the car she'd been driving, a late-model Toyota Celica. "Is that a rental?"

"No, it belonged to my mother. It's mine now."

He scrunched his brow, a bit confused. She'd mentioned getting a different car. "Are you going to ship it back to Hawaii?"

"No, I didn't reenlist. I'm living in Jeffersville now."

Clay hadn't seen that coming. She'd been so intent on staying in the Army. Had she changed her mind, hoping they could rekindle their relationship? If so, that made him feel all the worse.

He wasn't the man he used to be, although he hoped to be close to it one day soon. And while he wasn't the least bit opposed to making love with her again, he hated to see her give up her dreams. If that's what she'd done, then she was hoping for more than a physical relationship.

"You shouldn't have done it for me," he said.

She stiffened and took a step back. "I did it for *me*."

"I'm sorry. I didn't mean to make assumptions. It's just that…" He paused, trying to backpedal and not having much luck. "Then why are you here?"

She flinched as if he'd struck her.

Damn, he should have handled that better. "I'm sorry. I didn't mean to be a jerk. I guess my mood is only slightly better than it was the last time you saw me."

"You can say that again." She arched a pretty brow then slowly shook her head.

"I owe you an apology for that day, too. But keep in mind that I'd just gotten the worst news of my life, and I was in a lot of pain."

"You were also loaded down with pain medication, which can really take a toll on your thought process." Her downturned lips slowly curled into a pretty smile. "So you're forgiven."

He nodded, then pointed to the chair his mother had vacated. "Have a seat."

She seemed a bit reluctant. Then after a couple of beats, she complied. As she took the place beside him, she said, "I came to tell you something."

"What's that?"

She bit down on her bottom lip and paused for the longest time. Finally, she said, "I'm pregnant."

Wow. He had no idea what to say. He gave her expanded waistline another look, and when she rested her hand softly on a good-size baby bump, he realized now what he should have seen the moment she climbed out of her car.

He wasn't an expert on that sort of thing, but one of the guys in his unit had a pregnant wife. She'd been about seven months along and had a bump that size. And since he and Rickie had been together about five months ago, she must have been pregnant the day they'd met.

"I'm not asking anything of you," she said. "I can handle this on my own. But I thought you ought to know."

Why did she think he ought to…? Damn. No way. He'd used a condom. "Now wait a minute. Are you saying it's *mine*?"

"That's exactly what I'm saying." She turned toward him, her eyes zeroing in on his. She must have read the disbelief in them, because her gaze morphed into a glare. "Are you doubting me?"

He hadn't meant to be an ass about it, but yeah. He had plenty of doubts. Was she trying to pull something over on him?

It wouldn't be the first time a woman tried to snag

a soldier for his military benefits. And while Clay was no longer in the Army, his family did have a sizable spread that might seem appealing.

"It's just a little hard to believe," he said. "You look to be about six or seven months along."

"There's a good reason for that," Rickie said. "I'm carrying twins."

Clay wouldn't have been any more stunned if she'd doubled up her fist and bloodied his nose. *This couldn't be happening.*

Hell, if he didn't have a bum leg that ached like hell, he'd be tempted to take off at a dead run.

Before he could wrap his mind around the news or come up with any kind of response, the door squeaked open and his mother walked out, holding a tray filled with glasses of lemonade and several servings of cake.

At first, he thought she might have missed out on hearing the stunning announcement, but by the look on her face, he realized she'd heard at least part of it—the most shocking part. His mom loved babies and had mentioned a hundred times that she couldn't wait to be a grandma.

And that's when Clay realized he was in one hell of a fix.

Driving out to Wexler to visit Clay had been one of the dumbest decisions Rickie had ever made. And now he was looking at her as if she'd just set fire to her barn. She never should have come here today.

Okay, so he needed to know about the babies, but why hadn't she revealed her news the way she'd practiced? It had sounded so good when she stood in front of the bathroom mirror this morning and recited a script.

But when he asked why she was here, she figured she'd better cut to the chase. And that's when it all fell apart.

Rickie glanced at his mom. Poor Sandra gaped first at Clay, then at Rickie. This was *so* not going the way Rickie had planned.

Sandra leaned against the porch railing as if she might collapse. The tray she held was listing to the side, and if she wasn't careful, the drinks and the dessert were going to drop to the floor and make a terrible mess. Of course, that one would be a lot easier to clean up than the one Rickie had just created.

"Here," Rickie said, reaching for the tray. "Let me help you with that."

The dumbfounded woman, whose jaw had nearly dropped to the ground, handed it over without an argument. Then, after looking at Rickie's midsection, she snatched it right back again. "Good grief, you don't need to be helping me. Let me carry that."

Whatever. Rickie wasn't an invalid, but she decided not to argue. Instead, she tried to soften the blow and segue into a productive conversation. "I realize this is a bit of a shock."

"To say the least." Clay raked his hands through his hair, which had grown longer than his prior military cut.

She liked it that way, although she'd better not study him too closely. Like she'd told him before, she didn't need anything from him.

"I don't know what to say. This is more than a little mind-boggling." His expression verified his words.

"Don't worry," she told him. "I know you're not interested in having a relationship with me. And you don't need to have one with the babies, either. I just thought it was only right to let you know."

"You're pregnant with Clay's baby?" Sandra finally set the tray down on a small patio table. "I mean, *babies*? Oh my gosh. This is wonderful. I've always wanted to be a grandmother, but Clay insisted he wasn't going to ever have kids. So I'm delighted at the news. Do you know if you'll be having boys or girls?"

"Actually, there'll be one of each." Rickie glanced at Clay, who seemed too stunned to speak. "I'll admit that I was surprised, too. This wasn't something I expected to happen, but I'm making the best of it."

At that, Clay finally chimed in. "Okay, Mom. Would you mind giving Rickie and me a little privacy? We have some things to talk over, and we don't need an audience. Or a cheering section."

"Yes, of course." Sandra smiled brightly. "I'll just slip inside the house and find something to do."

Once the door clicked shut behind her, Rickie continued to stand, realizing she'd better not get too comfortable. "I didn't realize you don't like kids."

"It's not that. I just… Never mind."

"And I assume you're going to want a paternity test, but that won't be necessary. I'm not asking for child support." Rickie blew out a sigh. "But for the record, even though I was shocked and had to revamp my career plans, I'm actually happy about it. And that's why I'm no longer in the Army."

"I'd think you'd enjoy the security."

"Not if that meant being separated from my children for any length of time." She unfolded her arms. "Besides, I recently found a life insurance policy I didn't realize my parents had. So that'll tide me over for a while." A very short while.

"I don't know what to say." Clay shook his head, then reached down and rubbed his knee. "This isn't going to be easy for you."

"I don't expect it to be, but I've got things under control. I'm taking a couple of night classes, which will lead to a nursing degree. In the meantime, I'm job hunting. I hope to land a temporary position at a hospital or clinic until I have to go out on maternity leave. And actually, I have an interview at a local hospital in an hour, so I need to go."

"Before you do, how can I get a hold of you?"

She reached into her purse, pulled out a small notepad and pen. Then she jotted down her cell number and handed it to him. "I live in Jeffersville—on Bramble Berry Lane."

"Okay. Got it." He slipped the paper in his pocket. "Good luck on the interview."

"Thanks. I need a little time to unwind so I can put my best foot forward."

"You're not going to be able to work very long."

"It's a temporary position, but at least I can get my foot in the door there."

"So you plan to go to work after the babies are born?"

"That life insurance policy will be helpful for a while, but not until they go to kindergarten. So I'll have to get a job. But a lot of single moms are able to provide a loving home for their kids." She nodded toward her mother's car. "Anyway, I have to go."

As she opened the driver's door, he asked, "What are you going to do about child care?"

"I'm going to hire a nanny." She didn't wait for him to respond. Instead, she climbed into her car and headed for that interview.

She wasn't too worried about childcare. She had a couple of months to find a loving and dependable person to care for the twins.

It's just too bad they wouldn't have a loving and dependable daddy.

As Rickie drove away, Clay raked a hand through his hair and watched until her car disappeared from sight. Her unexpected visit had shocked the heck out of him, and her news had left him completely baffled. He had no idea what to think, let alone do.

He still couldn't believe what she'd just sprung on him. She was *pregnant*, and not with just one baby, but two. Even more surprising than that—according to her claim, he was the father.

Now that was rich. What did he know about babies or parenting? Then again, did he actually need those skills? Rickie had said she didn't need him or his financial support, which ought to be a relief. But it wasn't. What kind of guy turned his back on his kids?

He tried to sort through his thoughts, but guilt and confusion clouded his brain.

Apparently, fate wasn't finished messing with him. Could his life get any more unsettling?

When the screen door creaked open and his mother walked out onto the porch, he realized things were about to get worse.

She scanned the deserted yard and driveway. "Is Rickie gone?"

"Yeah." Clay kept his response simple, hoping his mom would just pick up that tray of drinks and cake and go back inside. He wasn't up for a discussion with anyone, especially his mom. But when she plopped down in the seat next to him, he knew he was in for a maternal interrogation.

Sandra Masters had never been able to read her only child, so she usually said the wrong thing or reacted in a way that made Clay clam up, rather than share his thoughts and feelings with her. And apparently, none of that had changed while he'd served in the Army.

She blew out a long, slow sigh. "So how are you feeling about all of this?"

"I'm in a state of shock."

"I can understand that."

Could she? He doubted it. She'd never really understood him or his need to set boundaries between them. Nor had she known how important it had been for him to join the military and do something noble with his life.

You'd think she'd realize that the military was in his blood. Hell, he'd been born on an Army base in Germany. His dad had been a career soldier who'd achieved valor in Desert Storm.

Clay didn't remember much about John Masters, other than he'd died in battle. Then eight years later, Clay and his mom moved to the Bar M, where the sprawling ranch house was filled with pictures and awards that memorialized his father, particularly his patriotism and valor.

She shouldn't have been surprised that he would want to be just like his dad. You'd think she would have been proud, but she wasn't. She'd been afraid of losing Clay, too.

But she'd lost him anyway. That damned flight mishap had taken the *real* Clay away from her for good, and she'd been left with a facsimile who was broken down and miserable.

"Rickie is a pretty girl," Mom said.

She certainly was. And if truth be told, he'd been glad to see her drive up—until she told him why she was here.

"She seems nice," Mom added. "Do you think she'll make a good mother?"

He hadn't expected the conversation to take a turn like that, but in spite of being a helicopter mom, Sandra Masters meant well.

"Believe it or not," he said, "I really don't know her very well. But she was an Army medic, and from what little I do know, she seems compassionate. I'm sure she'll be a good mother."

"So what do you plan to do?" Mom asked.

Okay, then. They were back to the issue at hand.

Clay scrubbed a hand over his chin. "Hell if I know. It sounds like she has life all figured out for herself and the kids."

I'm not asking anything of you, she'd said, more than once.

I can handle parenthood on my own.

"Maybe that was her way of trying to calm your fears and test the waters," his mom said.

That was possible, he supposed. No matter what Rickie had told him about her ability to go it alone, Clay would offer financial support.

Only trouble was, long before she'd made her announcement, he'd felt tied to the land and to civilian life. Taking on a daddy role would only serve to lock him down to the last place a guy like him wanted to be.

He might have gone to West Point and then served in the military, but there were some things that were part of a man's DNA. And Clay liked being a risk taker, liked pushing the limits and getting that adrenaline rush. And he was determined to somehow get his life back.

The doctors hadn't painted a rosy picture about him having a full recovery, but they didn't know him.

"I've been thinking," his mom said. "You should take some childbirth classes with her. And you should definitely go to one of her obstetrical appointments. Once you see those babies on an ultrasound, it'll make things real. And I have no doubt you'll fall in love with them and be an amazing father."

"Don't get carried away. This is all very new to me. Besides, Rickie and I didn't have an ongoing affair. Or a real relationship."

"Well, it looks as though the two of you will have one now. At least as parents."

And there lay the problem, considering the grump he'd been since that damn flight mishap. Try as he might, he hadn't been able to shake that dark mood in months. What made him think that he could turn that around before the baby…before the *babies* were born?

Twins. A boy and a girl. Who would have guessed that amazing night on a tropical beach would have produced two new human beings in one fell swoop?

Then again, Rickie said she'd been a twin herself. Multiple births ran in some families.

"Do you know how to find her?" his mom asked.

Clay patted his shirt pocket. "She gave me her contact info."

"I hope you won't wait too long. Those kids are going to need a mother *and* a father."

Clay had always been able to read the subtext behind her words. "And a grandmother, too. Right? Isn't that what this is all about?"

She clamped her lips together, realizing she'd shown her hand. And that, once again, she'd met her match.

Clay wasn't about to let her think she could push him into a relationship. Nor did he want her to continue with the false assumption that he'd eventually find something to make him happy he'd moved back to the ranch. That wasn't going to happen.

He loved his mom, but he'd be damned if he'd let her talk him into something he wasn't ready for. Hell, he hardly knew Rickie at all. He did, however, know her body intimately, and his thoughts drifted back to that night they'd met and their incredible lovemaking.

But there was more to a woman than a gorgeous face and a sexy body. He should probably get to know the *real* her better. Especially if she was having his babies.

He had no idea how she and the twins would fit into his life, though. But he wouldn't turn his back on them.

Still, what if the doctors had been wrong? What if his vision wouldn't remain impaired? When they'd explained the extent of his injuries, they'd used the word *likely* and not *definitely*. His leg was coming along well, and the physical therapist claimed he was making a lot more progress than most people with similar injuries. Maybe things wouldn't be as dire as they'd seemed when he'd been stretched out on that hospital bed at Tripler.

Clay blew out a sigh. Even if he could accept his limitations and his new normal, he wasn't prepared for fatherhood. Or any further loss of freedom.

But ready or not, that's where life was headed. And he wasn't the only one who'd be facing big changes. Rickie hadn't signed on for this, either.

He could make a slew of excuses for reacting to the news the way he had. After all, she'd just dumped it on him. And he'd never been comfortable with the touchy-feely stuff. But he probably should have been a little more sensitive, a little more understanding.

She hadn't seemed upset when she left. But then again, she hadn't been happy, either.

He reached into his pocket and pulled out the slip of paper Rickie had given him, making note of her ad-

Chapter Six

Clay spent most of the night tossing and turning, thanks to random thoughts of Rickie. He'd had several flashbacks of that day on the North Shore when she'd worn that sexy red bikini and that night she'd spent in his arms. He'd also envisioned her on the base, outside the clinic, her glossy brown hair pulled into a tight military bun.

He'd felt awkward talking to her that day, but the sight of her had spiked his interest, not to mention his hormones. And then he'd remembered the time she'd visited him in the hospital, compassion glimmering in her honey-brown eyes. In spite of her shy approach and her awkward attempt to offer support, he'd shut her out. He could come up with a boatload of excuses why he'd done it, but that didn't make it right.

mother him, which is why he usually fixed his own meals. "I'll just have bacon and toast."

"Are you sure? That's not going to help you regain the weight you lost."

Rather than comment, Clay glanced at the counter, where a dozen muffins rested on a cooling rack. They sure smelled good. Maybe he was hungrier than he thought.

He made his way to the kitchen table, which had been set for three. "Where's Granddad?"

"He's talking to the ranch hands and lining out their work for the day. He said he'd be back shortly."

Granddad, who'd always been tough as cowhide, loved working cattle. But he was in his late-seventies now, and Clay didn't want to see him push himself too hard. The old man should be thinking about retirement and not riding the range and supervising ranch hands. As soon as Clay was able to mount a horse and pull his own weight, he planned to take some of the load off his grandfather.

The mudroom door creaked open, and the silver-haired rancher strode into the house, his boot steps solid and steady in spite of his slight stoop.

"Well, look who's awake." Granddad winked at Clay, and his lips quirked into a smile. "It's Sleeping Beauty."

Clay wished that had been the case last night, but he wasn't going to offer a rebuttal that might require an explanation. Instead, he tossed his grandfather a wry grin. "It takes time for a body to heal, I guess. So I got a slow start this morning."

"I'm glad you're finally up. I've got a surprise for

you." Granddad crossed the room to the small desk near the pantry, opened a drawer and pulled out a piece of paper. "Life gave you one hell of a kick in the butt, so you might not appreciate this now, but one day you will."

"What's that?"

"Something I hope will soften the blow." Granddad handed over the paper, which appeared to be a legal document.

Clay scanned it, realizing he held the deed to the Bar M. And it no longer bore his grandfather's name.

"The ranch is all yours now," Granddad said.

Clay had never wanted to be tied to the land, but it was a generous gift, a loving one made from the heart. "I don't know what to say. 'Thank you' doesn't seem to be enough."

"That's good enough for me," Granddad said. "I realize you can't do much until you're back to fightin' weight, so I'll just continue to run the place till you're ready to take over."

"I'd appreciate that." Clay hoped to be able to take charge in a couple of weeks. He could probably do it now, but the last thing he needed to do was to screw up his leg before it was completely healed.

Call him crazy and a die-hard soldier, but he still hoped to be able to prove the military doctors wrong. He couldn't do a damn thing about the vision in his left eye, so he'd never be able to fly again. But he might be able to join the Texas National Guard. That way, he could still run the family ranch and serve the country for one weekend each month. It wouldn't be the same, ever, but it would still fulfill his dream. Sort of.

Granddad crossed the kitchen and snatched a crisp slice of bacon from the platter near the stove. Then he nodded toward the doorway. "I'm going to wash up."

When he left the kitchen, Clay was still holding the deed and studying his name. He was grateful and appreciative, but…well, now he felt more grounded than ever.

"Have you given Rickie and her situation any thought?" his mom asked.

"She's crossed my mind." Actually, he'd given her and her news a lot more thought than his mom would ever know. That's why he hadn't slept worth a damn.

His mother lowered the flame under the skillet and turned away from the stove to face him. "So what are you going to do?"

"I'm not sure yet." He had a good idea, though. A starting point. But he didn't want to go into any real detail until he'd thought through all the possible repercussions. "There's a lot to consider."

She nodded, as if she understood. "Can I pour you a cup of coffee?"

"That sounds good. But I'll take it to go."

At that, her brow furrowed. "Where are you going? You had physical therapy yesterday."

He might regret the revelation later, but for some reason, he decided to be more open with her than usual. "I'm going to Jeffersville. I need to talk to Rickie."

Mom's bright smile lit her blue eyes in a way he hadn't seen in a long time. "That's a good idea."

He sure hoped so. Either way, he couldn't ignore

the situation. He preferred to address problems head-on, and this one would be no different, even though fatherhood would complicate his life in ways he couldn't imagine.

While his mom poured coffee into an insulated disposable cup, he glanced at the clock on the microwave. It was too early to show up unexpectedly at Rickie's house. But he wasn't about to remain on the ranch, where his mom was sure to throw in her good-hearted two cents every chance she got.

He'd figure out a way to stall for time, even if that meant he had to drive around Jeffersville and check out the town where Rickie lived and would raise the twins.

Maybe by then, he would come up with a way to get on her good side, especially since he had a feeling she'd be offended if he insisted upon having a paternity test.

Rickie had driven away from the Bar M yesterday wishing she'd never made the trek to Wexler. Yet at the same time, she was glad she could finally put the much-needed conversation with Clay behind her.

She'd guessed the news of her pregnancy would surprise him, and she'd been right. It hadn't pleased him, either. But what had she expected? There was no way he'd feel the same way about the babies that she did. Hopefully, after he had a chance to absorb it all, he'd be more accepting. But even if that didn't turn out to be the case, she'd make out okay on her own.

When she'd told him she had to leave for a job interview, she hadn't been blowing smoke. The temp agency she was working with had set up an appointment for her to meet with Dr. Glory Davidson at a family practice clinic in Brighton Valley.

The doctor had a two-month position for a receptionist. And by the time Rickie arrived, she'd rallied her emotions so she could put her best foot forward.

And it worked. Rickie and the fortysomething physician seemed to hit it off from the get-go. The doctor led Rickie back to her office and pointed to a chair in front of her desk, indicating that Rickie should sit down. Then she took her seat. "Call me Glory," she said. "We're pretty casual around here."

That might be true, but there'd been no sign that they were lax. The clinic was clean and orderly. And Glory, who wore a white lab coat over a light blue blouse and black slacks, was dressed professionally.

"My receptionist has family living in Mexico," Glory said, "and her father recently had a crippling stroke. So she's taking some time off to care for him and help him get settled in a rehab facility. We can get by without her for a few days to a week, but it looks like she'll be gone two months or more."

"The timing works for me," Rickie said. "My babies aren't due until late February."

Glory leaned forward and rested her forearms on her desk. "I like the fact that you were a medic. And, by the way, thank you for your service."

Rickie merely nodded. She never quite knew what to say to people who thanked her for doing the work she'd loved.

"Lorena does a great job answering the phone and scheduling appointments," Glory said, "but she doesn't have any medical training. So you'll be a nice addition to the office, especially since you can take vitals and draw blood."

"I'm a certified EMT," Rickie said. "And I'm a fast learner."

"That's good to know." Glory leaned back in her desk chair, the springs creaking. "Are you available to start work on Monday morning?"

"Yes, I can."

Glory studied her a moment, then asked, "Have you ever thought about going to nursing school?"

"Actually, that's been a dream of mine. I'm not sure how I'll pull that off once the twins get here. They'll keep me busy. Plus I'll also need a full-time job in order to support us. So school will have to wait. In the meantime, I'd love to work in the medical field, even if it's as a paramedic."

"Lorena mentioned something about retiring next fall," Glory said. "So a permanent position here at the clinic might open up at the right time for you."

"That would be perfect," Rickie said. "And just so you know, I plan to start interviewing nannies before the twins are born. I'll find someone dependable."

"I have four kids of my own, so I know what it's like to work around the physical limitations of pregnancy. I've also had to deal with an occasional child-care issue. I'm pretty flexible, so I don't foresee any problems."

Rickie came away from the interview feeling good about the temporary job she'd landed. Glory Davidson was personable, and since she seemed to be understanding of a single mother's plight, it looked like it might be a good fit.

The only downside was the forty-five-minute commute, which would get tiring after a while. And if it turned into a permanent position, she'd be away from the babies an extra hour and a half each day.

It was too bad she couldn't find something closer. But she wasn't too worried. She'd found this position easily, so if things didn't work out, she might not have any trouble finding something else closer to the house.

The drive home from the clinic would have gone quickly, but Rickie had spotted a children's shop located near the interstate and had decided to stop. After nearly an hour spent checking out cribs, bedding and baby clothes, she finally drove back to her house. All the while, she made a mental note of everything she wanted to accomplish prior to her due date. Then before going to bed, she wrote out a long to-do list scheduling her priorities.

Over the years, she'd learned that organization and having a solid game plan were key, so she woke up the next morning energized and ready to get started. Her biggest job was to convert her father's home office into a nursery, which would take a while since she had to empty it first.

While getting dressed, she studied her image in the full-length mirror that hung on her bedroom door. She caressed her baby bump, which seemed to grow bigger every day. She wondered what it would look like four months from now.

A slow grin stole across her lips. As long as the little ones were healthy and she carried them to term, she didn't mind if she got as big as a barn.

She chose to wear a pair of stretchy workout pants and an oversize shirt for comfort and mobility. Then she pulled her hair into a messy topknot so the long, curly strands wouldn't get in her way while she worked.

She'd no more than left her bedroom and stepped into the hall when the doorbell rang. She couldn't imagine who it might be, but she wouldn't know until she answered. So she padded to the door.

The moment she spotted Clay on the stoop, wearing a sheepish grin that dimpled his cheeks, her breath caught. Talk about surprise visits.

His hair was stylishly mussed. Gone was the Army captain, she thought. His appearance alone darn near screamed cowboy—and much more than it had yesterday when he'd been at the ranch.

She took in his chambray shirt, with the sleeves rolled up to his muscular forearms, the worn denim jeans and scuffed boots, then scanned back up to his handsome face. The only sign of his injury was a scar over his left brow.

"What are you doing here?" she asked.

"I had some time to mull over what you told me yesterday, and I thought I'd better come here and talk to you in person."

She continued to stand there, unable to move, while gawking at him and wishing she'd been better prepared for his arrival.

"Aren't you going to invite me in?" he asked.

At that, she finally came to her senses. "Yes, sure.

Of course. Come on in." She stepped aside, letting him enter the small living room, then closing the door.

"Nice house," he said, checking out the interior. "Did you grow up here?"

"I… No, not exactly. We moved here when I was in high school." It's not as if she had any real attachment to the house, but she was glad to have a place to raise her babies.

"I hope I didn't come too early," Clay said. "I was afraid I might wake you up."

"No, I've been up for a while."

Should she offer him something to eat or drink? That might make it easier for him to say whatever he had on his mind.

"I can make a pot of coffee," she said, "but I only have decaf. I also have orange juice."

"Thanks, but I'm fine. I had breakfast at a diner near the interstate." He shoved his thumbs in the front pockets of his jeans. "How'd your interview go yesterday?"

"Much better than I'd hoped. I start work at a clinic in Brighton Valley on Monday. It's only a temporary position, and the pay isn't much, but there's a chance I could land a permanent job there in the future."

"You don't mind the long drive to work?"

She shrugged. "I'm not happy about it. But there are other options."

"Like what?"

"I could find a rental house in Brighton Valley and rent this one out. Or I could sell this house and buy another."

He arched a brow, then nodded as if her plan made

perfect sense. Did he realize a move to Brighton Valley would put her closer to his ranch?

He glanced at her expanding belly. "What about the babies?"

"I'll take it one day at a time. I've never been a single mother before."

"I'm sorry," he said.

"About what?" That she'd ended up pregnant after their lovemaking? That he'd practically shunned her when she visited him at Tripler when she'd been worried about him and had only wanted to offer her sympathy?

"About yesterday. It's just that… Well, let's just say that your pregnancy announcement knocked me off balance."

"I knew it would. I didn't expect you to be happy about it, either. In fact, I considered not telling you at all, but that wouldn't have been right."

"I'm glad you told me. To be completely honest, I wasn't happy. But after sleeping on it, I feel a little better about things now."

"I don't blame you for needing some time to think things over. I showed up unexpectedly and hit you with some pretty surprising news. Not only am I pregnant, but I'm having two babies."

"I guess twins run in your family."

"Apparently so." That was another reason she was happy about the pregnancy. The whole idea of having twins reminded her of the sister she'd lost, the closeness they'd shared in spite of Lainie's frail health.

Neither of them spoke for a moment. Then she added, "I'm going to call the girl Elena, after my sister."

"What about the boy?"

"I haven't decided." There really wasn't anyone in her family that she'd want to honor. She'd never really liked her adoptive father's name and wouldn't want to call her son Edwin, which sounded too old. And her biological dad hadn't been the kind of man she'd want her son to emulate.

Would Clay offer up a suggestion? Did he have a friend or family member he wanted to honor?

Then again, he'd come here to apologize for his attitude yesterday. And he wasn't exactly offering to take on a paternal role, which was fine with her.

They continued to stand in the middle of the living room, both pensive and silent.

Finally, Clay said, "Just for the record, I plan to pay you child support. I'd just… Well, I don't want this to sound mean or anything, but I'd like to have a DNA test first."

The comment hurt, and she flinched ever so slightly. She understood why he'd want paternity proven, but it also questioned her honesty and integrity. But then again, he really didn't know her.

"I'm sorry," he said again. "It's not that I don't trust or believe you. It's just…a formality. And I think it will protect everyone involved."

"I understand." She had to admit that she really couldn't blame him.

"And that's another reason I'm here. Under the circumstances, I think we should get to know each other better."

Now that surprised her. And oddly enough, it pleased her, too. "What did you have in mind?"

In all honesty, Clay hadn't thought it out that far. Rickie flinched when he'd mentioned that he wanted a paternity test, which the family lawyer was going to insist upon. He had no reason to doubt her words or her determination to go it alone, but he caught something hiding in her expressive brown eyes, a secret she harbored beneath the surface.

For a brief moment, sadness and vulnerability stole across her face, mocking everything she'd just told him. And even if she could handle it on her own, she shouldn't have to.

So he'd suggested they spend some time getting to know each other to soften the blow, especially today, when she stood before him, alone and vulnerable, yet proud, wearing curve-hugging stretch pants and a blousy green top that suggested she planned to work out.

"We could start by going out to lunch," he said. "What do you think?"

His suggestion must have taken her aback, because she didn't say anything right away. When she finally spoke, she asked, "When do you want to do that?"

Not today, he supposed. It wasn't even close to noon. "What about one day next week?"

"I start work on Monday, so we'd have to find a place for a quick meal in Brighton Valley."

"Actually, that would work better for me anyway." The moment the words rolled off his tongue, he regretted them. This wasn't about *him* or his convenience.

Well, in a way, he supposed it was. If he didn't look out for his best interests, who would?

Still, all of his self-talk failed to do the trick because, when push came to shove, he believed her claim. And that meant those babies would prove to be his.

So now what? She'd invited him inside, but she hadn't asked him to have a seat. Should he sit down anyway?

He'd come to see her today, hoping to get on her good side, but so far his efforts didn't seem to be working very well. He ought to be happy that she'd agreed to meet him for lunch in Brighton Valley next week. But she'd probably only have an hour, which wouldn't give them much time to talk.

Instead of waiting for an invitation to make himself at home, he took a couple steps forward and scanned the cozy living room once more, thinking that the decor was scarce compared to his family home, a sprawling five-bedroom ranch house loaded down with colorful, handwoven rugs on the hardwood floors, southwestern artwork on the walls and tons of photographs throughout.

He spotted several cardboard boxes in a corner, next to a stack of framed pictures, and it struck him that she might be moving. Apparently she'd been serious about leasing out her house and finding a rental in Brighton Valley.

"What's going on with that stuff over there?" he asked. "Are you moving in or out?"

"A little of both." She chuckled softly, which was the first sign that they might be able to get through the initial awkwardness of his unannounced visit. "After my parents died, I packed up the house and put some of their personal things in storage. The plan was to either sell the house or rent it out furnished. And now that I'm home to stay, I've been bringing things back and putting them where they belong."

"I'd be happy to help."

"That's not necessary."

She'd told him she wasn't going to ask anything of him, and apparently she meant it. That further convinced him that she was telling the truth, that he'd fathered those babies. She also seemed determined to handle things on her own. Didn't that prove that she wasn't like Tyrone's ex-wife and that she wasn't trying to put something over on him?

He slowly shook his head and stepped forward. Using his best commanding officer's voice, he said, "You shouldn't be lifting boxes. Or reaching up to hang pictures. I'll do it for you. Just tell me where you want them."

Rickie folded her arms, resting them on top of her baby bump. "I didn't have any problem bringing them in from storage. And they can stay right where they are."

"I've got a couple of hours," he said. "You might as well put me to work."

She sucked in a deep breath, then slowly blew it out. "I planned to go through those boxes and take out what I'd like to keep in the house. The rest of the stuff can go out in the garage."

"Okay, so sorting stuff is something you'll have to do yourself. But I'm here now. What else can I do?"

She studied him for a moment, as if questioning the

wisdom of allowing him into her home and into her life. Then she uncrossed her arms. "I'm clearing out the office so I can convert it into a nursery. I realize I have time to get that done, but I'd feel better if I had things ready way before the babies get here. My doctor said that twins often come early."

"Then you may as well give me a list of things to do. In a few weeks, I won't be as available as I am now."

She bit down on her bottom lip, as if pondering the wisdom of accepting his help. Finally, she said, "I do need to move the office furniture into the garage."

"All right. And after that…?"

She scrunched her pretty face and placed her hands on her hips. "You're serious about this."

"You bet I am." He just hoped he wouldn't live to regret it.

"Do you know how to paint?" she asked.

"I've had plenty of experience painting the barn and the corrals on the ranch. Why?"

"The walls are white now and a little dingy, so I want to freshen things up and change to something more bright and cheerful." Rickie pointed toward the hallway. "Come on. I'll show it to you and tell you what I have in mind for the nursery."

Clay followed her past an open bedroom door and to the office. The room was pretty empty, other than the furniture—a desk, a wheeled chair, a small bookshelf and a metal file cabinet.

"Once this room is cleared," she said, "I'd like to paint the walls light green. And if I can remember how to use my mom's sewing machine, I'll try to make some curtains with a cute animal print. Or maybe I'll just put a valance on top of some new white blinds."

She was nesting and clearly more content with the life changes coming her way than Clay was. Not that he found anything wrong with that. Creating a home for the twins was a good thing. Kids needed a loving mother.

They needed a father, too, he supposed. Although he'd learned to live without one. Of course, Granddad had stepped into that position when Clay was a teenager, clamping down on him occasionally, but only when Clay got too rebellious. For the most part, Granddad had a boys-will-be-boys attitude, but he knew how to yell and cuss. And he knew how to set limits.

But even though Granddad might have set a good example of how to be a disciplinarian, babies needed a gentle hand. And Clay suspected he'd fall short when it came to being a nurturer.

"I'm going to put one crib against the east wall," Rickie explained. "And the other one will go near the closet. I think I can get by with a single chest of drawers. At least, for the time being."

He hadn't thought about that. She was going to need a lot of baby stuff. And two of most things. That was going to be costly. He'd have to make a financial contribution toward her purchases.

After she took him to the garage and pointed out the spot where she wanted to store the office furniture, he returned to the house and began moving things. He thought about driving back to the ranch to get a dolly, but that was going to take a while. And he hated to have her think he was wimping out on her.

The file cabinet was empty, which made it easy for one guy to move alone. And the bookshelf was fairly light. The desk, on the other hand, was going to be more challenging. But he was strong and industrious. Besides, it wasn't that big. When he'd been in high school, he'd had one about that same size in his bedroom.

"I can help you move that," she said.

"The heck you will." He shot her a you've-got-to-be-kidding-me look and rolled his eyes. "I got it."

Determined to prove himself and to show her that he wasn't an invalid, he kicked aside a large throw rug that had been sitting in front of it. Then he pulled the desk away from the wall. He stepped back, thinking he might use that rug to his advantage. The plan was to set it under the two rear legs, then slide the desk across the floor.

As he spun to the right, he tripped over the damn thing, lost his balance and dropped to the hardwood floor.

It all happened so quickly, he couldn't do a single thing to correct his fall. As he landed on his bad knee, a sharp pain sliced to the bone. "Dammit."

"Oh, no." Rickie rushed to his side and dropped to the floor. "Are you all right?"

No. He hurt like hell. And so did his pride.

"I'm okay," he said as he slowly rolled to the side, taking the weight off his knee, and sat on his butt. Then he stretched out his leg, which throbbed and ached like a son of a gun.

"I just need to take the weight off it for a while." Actually, he was more concerned about the long-term effect of his fall. He'd hate to suffer a setback in his rehab. But he didn't say a word about that. Otherwise, she'd probably run him off and try to do the heavy work on her own.

As Rickie knelt beside him, the alluring scent of her shampoo, something that smelled like tropical fruit, filled his head, offering him a temporary distraction. Then she gently probed his knee. "I was afraid something like this might happen. I'll get you an ice pack."

"That's not necessary. It feels better already." Hell, just her TLC was enough to take the edge off the pain.

Apparently she wasn't convinced, because she continued to finger his knee.

He tried to make light of the situation and tossed her a crooked grin. "I guess you can take the medic out of the Army, but you can't take the medic's heart out of the girl."

She blessed him with a pretty smile, and the soreness faded even more. Time stalled, then rolled back, taking him to a different place, one where the waves splashed on the shore, where the scent of sunblock filled the warm, tropical air.

The recollection was so real it spiked his hormones, and a blast of heat shot through his veins. Without a thought to the repercussions, he reached up and cupped her jaw.

Her lips parted at the unexpected touch, and as their eyes met, he brushed his thumb across her cheek, caressing her skin. Memories of that romantic Hawaiian night built into a tropical storm, stirring up the same sweet pheromones that first surfaced while they'd sat on the sand and watched the sun go down.

He had half a notion to…

No, that was *crazy*. He wasn't about to follow up on a sexual compulsion like that. He already knew what making love with her was like. And there was more to life than great sex.

Instead of going to bed and allowing their physical needs to be met, they ought to spend time together, talking and getting to know each other.

He removed his hand and glanced away, breaking eye contact before he completely lost his head. "I think I'd better leave that desk where it is for now. I'll come back with some tools and take it apart. That way it'll be easier to move."

"I'm sure you have other things to do," she said. "And it's a long drive back to the ranch."

"I saw a hardware store not far from here. I'll just go pick up a screwdriver and a wrench. It'll just take a few minutes."

"I appreciate this, but you really don't have to help me."

He knew that. Only trouble was, he actually wanted to.

Chapter Seven

"You had a funny look on your face when I asked if I could go with you," Rickie told Clay as they made their way to the curb in front of her house, where he'd parked his truck. "Are you sure you don't mind if I tag along?"

"No, not at all. I was just a little surprised that you want to go to a hardware store."

"I want to pick up some paint samples to take with me when I go shopping for the baby bedding and the material for curtains."

"Wow. You're really getting into the whole decorating thing."

Apparently, she'd surprised him yet again. But when she glanced his way to read his expression, he tossed her a grin. Then they both got into the truck, and he started the engine.

Ten minutes later, they arrived at Hadley's Building Supplies on the outskirts of Jeffersville. As they walked toward the entrance, Rickie took a moment to watch Clay's gait, noting that his limp was more pronounced than when he'd first arrived at her house.

"You probably should have kept that ice pack on your leg longer," she said.

He shook his head. "Nah. I'm doing okay."

She wasn't sure if he was being truthful or macho. With some men, it was hard to say. But she decided to take him at his word.

When they'd gotten about six feet from the door, a little red-haired boy breezed by Rickie, practically cutting her off and causing her to trip and stumble.

Clay reached out to steady her, his grip on her arm firm.

"Mikey!" a woman cried out. "I did *not* give you permission to run ahead. Apologize to that lady, then come back here."

The boy, who was about four or five, was a cute kid, even with hair that stood up on one side, freckles sprinkled across his face and a smudge of dirt marring his chin. He bit down on his bottom lip, then looked at Rickie and frowned. "Sorry, lady."

"Apology accepted." Rickie offered him a smile, then glanced at the woman who'd called him back, assuming she was his mother. She was in her midthirties with shoulder-length dark hair and a baby bump that suggested she was due to deliver anytime. She also looked a bit worn and frazzled, no doubt from chasing after the energetic little boy all morning long.

If Rickie had been alone, she would have spoken to her and asked when her baby was due. She'd also ask the woman if she was having a boy or a girl, but Rickie wasn't about to let her maternal hormones run away with her while she was with Clay.

When he opened the door for her, she stepped inside, followed by Mikey and his mom.

"If you're good," the mother told her son, "I'll buy you candy to eat on the way home."

A sugar rush was the last thing that kid needed, but Rickie kept that thought to herself.

Clay pointed to the right. "There's the tool section."

Rickie followed him down the aisle.

"That poor lady has her hands full," Clay said. "And it looks like she's going to have another one to chase after before she knows it."

Rickie agreed, but she didn't comment. She was going to have her hands full soon, too. How did Clay feel about that? Would he offer to help out? Or would he steer clear of her?

She tried to read between the lines, to gauge the subtext behind his words. But she decided to take one day at a time. He was here with her now. And he'd offered to paint the nursery.

Clay stopped in front of a display of packaged household sets that included several pastel-colored tools, including a couple of screwdrivers, a small hammer and a pair of pliers. They were kind of cute and probably functional. But they looked a little too girly to her.

"My dad's tools are in storage, so it seems like a waste of money to buy new ones." Rickie would have suggested they go look for them, but she hadn't labeled the boxes, so it would take a long time to find them.

"I could drive back to the Bar M and pick up my screwdrivers, too. But I don't feel like making that trek, especially if it sets me back a few hours. So this will get the job done." He bypassed the pink set and chose one that was Tiffany blue in color. "Consider it a house-warming gift. You can keep them in the kitchen for little jobs that might come up. Besides, you're having two babies. There's no telling how often they'll break something and you'll have to fix it."

"Are you suggesting the twins will be as active and impulsive as Mikey?"

"Yep. If they grow up to be anything like the kid I used to be, you will." He winked, then tucked the tool set under his arm.

She thanked him, even though she didn't see the need to have girly tools. But a wrench by any color was still a wrench, right? And if she faced a bigger repair job, she'd call a handyman.

"Now let's go find those color samples," he said.

They continued to the paint section and stopped in front of a rack that displayed a variety of options. She immediately looked for a pale green, which would match the comforter set she'd seen while shopping yesterday. She'd liked the jungle animal print, especially the cute monkeys in the trees. She'd also spotted one with a Western theme that boasted little red barns, brown ponies and cowgirls and cowboys spinning lariats. If she ended up buying that one, she'd probably want beige walls.

She glanced at Clay, who stood patiently beside her, looking all tall and lean and cowboy. He barely resembled the handsome, bare-chested guy who'd charmed her on the beach or the skilled lover who'd made her feel like the only woman in the world. But Bullet by any other name was still Bullet. Right?

The chemistry they'd shared in bed was certainly still there. Just minutes ago, while seated on the floor of the office—or rather, the nursery—he'd nearly kissed her.

She'd seen the heat in his eyes, just as she'd spotted it when they'd slow danced on the sand and again in that rented bungalow. She'd sympathized with him when he'd tripped and landed on his knee, but while she'd examined him, something sparked between them, and she'd been sorely tempted to instigate that kiss herself, which would have been stupid.

Like he'd said, they didn't know each other very well. And it wasn't a good idea to let lust run away with them.

She removed a sample that had several shades of light green, as well as one with several beige hues, and showed them to Clay. "What do you think?"

"Does it matter?"

For some crazy reason, it did. "I'm still trying to decide on the decor for the nursery. I'm torn between animals and cowboys."

A smile tugged at his lips. "I'm sure you'll make the right decision."

Yes, eventually she would, but it would be nice if he took more of an interest in her decorating choices.

"You mentioned green when we were in the office," he said. "So it sounds like you've already decided."

"Good point." She replaced the brown sample, then held up the other to the artificial light, as if it might help her check the color variances. But more than that, she also wanted to know which shade matched his green eyes.

That way, if he didn't come around very often, she had something in the nursery that would remind her of him. Of course, she'd also have the babies in their beds.

"Is there anything else you want to see here?" he asked.

"No, this is good for now." Painting the nursery was just the first step in preparing for the twins. She'd also have to buy two cribs and a chest of drawers.

From a couple of aisles over, a familiar voice rang out. "Mikey! Where did you run off to?"

Rickie couldn't help but smile. Obviously, Mikey had forgotten about the candy bribe his mom had promised him.

"Michael Allen Weldon," she called out again. "Did you hear me? I'm not playing games. And I'm not buying that candy. If you don't get over here right now, you're going to lose television privileges for a week."

"Sounds like she means business," Clay said.

"No," the boy cried out. *"Not* the TV. I'm comin', Mama."

"Attaboy," Clay said. "Smart kid."

Rickie stole a glance at the gorgeous man walking beside her, the father of her babies. Would he be a good one? Would he play an active paternal role?

Cut it out, Rickie. Do you really want him that involved in your life, in the decisions you make?

Maybe, she thought.

Or would that merely complicate things? What if he got too involved while coparenting? Or too opinionated?

There were some good things to be said about being a single mother, she supposed. She wouldn't have to answer to anyone but herself.

As they reached the end of the paint aisle, they turned to the right, toward the registers, and she caught a blur in her peripheral vision right before she felt a hard thud on her thigh. Mikey bounced off her leg and fell to the floor in front of her, just in time for her to trip over him.

She gasped. If Clay hadn't reached out to catch her, she might have fallen to the floor. Or worse, landed on top of the little rascal, who sat on the floor, his eyes wide at the near mishap, his legs stretched out in front of him and his cowboy boots on the wrong feet.

"Sorry," Mikey said, as he jumped up and dashed off to find his mother.

"Are you okay?" Clay asked as he slipped his arm around her waist and held her steady.

"I think so." She placed her hand protectively over her baby bump, which had become a habit lately. "I'm glad I didn't step on that little guy."

Clay's brow furrowed, and he held her tighter. "And I'm glad you didn't fall and hurt yourself."

"Me, too." She should have been paying attention to where she was walking and not focusing on the attractive cowboy she was with.

As they checked out, she opened her purse to pull out a credit card, but Clay waved her off. "I got this. Remember?"

The housewarming gift. Should she argue? Or just let it ride?

Clay Masters was an enigma, and she had no idea what to do about him. But she'd better figure out something before they got home. His visit had come out of the blue. And she had a feeling she'd better brace herself so he wouldn't knock her completely off balance, just like Mikey. Only this fall would be a lot harder.

Clay stayed at Rickie's house until four o'clock that afternoon. He'd only meant to take apart the desk, carry the pieces out to the garage and then put it back together again. But by the time he'd finished that task and re-entered the kitchen, she was making sandwiches and cutting up fresh fruit.

"I made lunch for us," she'd said. "I still get a little nauseous if I go too long on an empty stomach."

So how could he say no?

After they ate, he carried a few boxes in from the car and stacked them in the dining room for her to sort through later. When he spotted her dragging out a ladder so she could replace the bulbs in the overhead lights, he'd insisted that she let him do it.

Needless to say, he stayed longer than he'd planned. After the forty-five-mile drive, he arrived home at the dinner hour. Fortunately, he'd been able to ward off the maternal interrogation until he sat down at the family table.

"So," Mom said as she passed Clay the mashed potatoes. "How did things go today?"

"All right." He spooned a large helping onto his plate, then passed the bowl to Granddad.

"You were gone a long time," she said. "Were you with Rickie all day?"

"A couple hours." Actually, it was more like seven, but if he admitted that, she'd never stop quizzing him.

"I hope she's feeling well," Mom added.

"She seems to be." Other than the nausea that still plagued her at times. At least, that's the conclusion he'd come to.

"Would someone pass the gravy?" Granddad said, offering a welcome distraction from the line of questioning. He'd often done the same thing when Clay had been in high school. Once, when Clay thanked him for running interference for him at times, his grandfather winked at him, his eyes sparkling with mirth, and said, "I ain't so old that I don't remember what it was like to be young. Just make sure you stay safe—and obey the law."

For the most part, Clay and his buddies had tried to do that.

Mom reached for the gravy bowl but never missed a beat. "Is Rickie seeing a doctor regularly?"

"I assume she is. She knows the importance of good medical care."

"That's good to know," Mom said. "There can be pregnancy complications, especially with women carrying multiples."

Clay stiffened and scrunched his brow. "What kind of complications?"

"High blood pressure, preeclampsia, premature labor…"

Damn. He hadn't considered health risks.

"Are her parents supportive?" Mom asked, clearly not able to quell her curiosity.

"They were in a car accident and passed away about six months ago."

"Oh, no. I'm sorry to hear that. Does she have a sister or friend who'll be with her during the delivery?"

Clay had no idea. Nor had he considered she might need emotional support as well as financial. But the more he thought about it, the more concerned he grew. "I'm not sure."

"I can understand your reluctance to get too involved," his mom said. "You probably should move slowly."

"Agreed."

Still, he had to admit that he'd learned a few things about Rickie today. She had an independent streak he hadn't realized, a take-charge attitude. And something told him that his kids, assuming those babies were actually his, would be in good hands.

Of course, that wouldn't absolve him from taking responsibility. He'd figure out a way to help her with those babies. Hopefully he could do that without making any kind of commitment that might suck the life out of him.

"Would you mind if I talked to her?"

Taken aback by the question, Clay's first impulse was to tell his mother to back off. But on the other hand, he didn't like the idea of Rickie facing labor and delivery alone. Women usually needed each other at times like that, especially if there were complications.

If his mother reached out to her, maybe Clay would feel better about setting up some boundaries. Because if he didn't, he'd find himself getting sucked into her world—and even more tied down than he already was.

"Sure," he said. "I'll give you her number."

Three days later, Clay wished he'd kept that information to himself. Not only had his mother called Rickie, but before *he* could set up a lunch date with Rickie, the two women had made plans to meet at Caroline's Diner in Brighton Valley on Wednesday at noon!

Which was why Clay decided to crash that luncheon before his mom became way more involved than necessary.

Rickie had been so stunned when Sandra Masters called and asked her to meet for lunch in Brighton Valley that a response knotted up in her throat. It had taken her a couple of beats to finally be able to speak.

Sandra had obviously gotten Rickie's number from Clay, which meant he was okay with it, so she'd agreed to meet on Wednesday. That gave her time to get a feel for the clinic schedule and to find out when she'd be able to take a lunch break.

She talked to Sandra again last night, and they made plans to meet in front of a place called Caroline's Diner at ten minutes past noon.

Rickie was a bit nervous, although Sandra had been so sweet on the telephone that it seemed silly to stress about it. Besides, spending some time with Clay's mother also meant she'd learn more about her children's father—and his family.

The diner was located on the shady main drag, not far from the town square and the family clinic where she worked. So she'd found it easily enough.

She'd no more than opened the front door when she spotted Sandra, who was already waiting near the old-style register.

The petite blonde in her late fifties quickly got up from her seat and greeted Rickie with a smile. "They don't take reservations, but I wanted to get here early to make sure they could seat us. This place really fills up around mealtime."

Rickie scanned the interior of the small-town eatery, noting the pale yellow walls and white café-style curtains on the front windows. "What a darling restaurant."

"Isn't it? And the food is to die for. If you like home-style cooking, you won't find a better meal than here. And Caroline makes the best desserts you've ever tasted. Check this out." Sandra pointed to a refrigerator display case that sat next to the cash register. It was chock-full of homemade goodies.

Rickie was drawn to a three-layer carrot cake, although the lemon meringue pie looked yummy, too. She usually tried to stay away from sweets, but she might have to make an exception today.

Sandra motioned to a matronly waitress who wore her graying dark hair in a topknot. "We're both here now, Margie."

The ruddy-faced waitress broke into a bright-eyed grin. "I'll have that booth ready for you in just a minute."

While waiting to be seated, Rickie glanced at a blackboard, on which someone had written What the Sheriff Ate in yellow chalk. Just underneath, it read, Baked Ham, Scalloped Potatoes, Glazed Carrots and Apple Pie à la Mode—$9.95.

"Caroline's husband is retired now," Sandra explained, "but he was once the only law enforcement officer in Brighton Valley. She and everyone else still refer to him as the sheriff. And that's how she announces her daily specials."

"What a clever idea. I like that." In fact, there was a lot Rickie liked about Brighton Valley. The diner sat along a quaint, tree-lined street that was the perfect place for a lazy walk—and some shopping.

She'd arrived a few minutes earlier than the time she and Sandra had agreed to meet, just so she could take a quick walking tour of downtown Brighton Valley. And she was glad she did. Just across the street and down a couple of doors, she'd noticed a real estate office. Not that she planned to relocate right away. She'd only worked two and a half days at the clinic, but she liked Glory. And if that permanent position opened up, she'd be tempted to sell her house and move.

"Your table's ready," Margie called out as she waved Sandra and Rickie to a corner booth at the back of the diner.

Sandra was the first to slide onto the brown vinyl seat. Before Rickie joined her, she noticed Margie giving her a once-over.

"You new in town?" Margie asked. "Or just visiting?"

"I don't actually live in Brighton Valley, but I got a temp job that started here on Monday morning."

"Oh, yeah? Who do you work for? I know just about everyone in these parts."

"Dr. Davidson."

"Good deal." Margie broke into a big grin. "Glory Davidson is the best darn doctor in the world, if you ask me. I've been going to her ever since she took over ol' Doc McCoy's practice. Are you covering for Lorena? The poor thing had to go back to Mexico to check on her daddy."

Rickie's only response was to nod as she slid into the booth next to Sandra.

"When is your baby due?" Margie asked.

"February 28."

Margie let out a whistle. "I thought you were going to say it was due around Christmas. You must be having a big baby."

"She's having twins," Sandra said, her eyes lighting up.

Margie brightened, and she clapped her hands together like a happy child. "How exciting. I always wanted to have a set of twins. That is, until I had my firstborn, Jimmy Lee. That boy was as cute as a bug, but a real pistol. By the time he hit the terrible twos, I was so grateful that I only had one of him."

Sandra laughed. "My son, Clay, was like that, too. A real handful."

Margie gave them two menus, took their drink orders, then left them to chat.

Sandra leaned forward and lowered her voice. "Margie is a sweetheart, but she's a bit nosy and prone to repeat things she's heard."

Rickie nodded, although she'd already figured that out on her own. Still, she couldn't help but like the server's friendly nature.

"Anyway," Sandra said, "thanks for meeting me today. I thought it would be nice if we got to know each other better."

Rickie offered her a smile. Clay was the one she really wanted to know better, but his mom seemed nice. And learning more about her and his family would be helpful.

"I know Jeffersville is a bit of a drive from Wexler, but it's closer than if you were still on an Army base in Honolulu. At least we can visit once in a while. I'd like to get to know my grandchildren. And you, too, of course."

"I would have reenlisted, but when I found out I was pregnant, I realized that if I was deployed, I wouldn't have anyone to watch the babies for me."

"Clay mentioned you lost your parents recently. I'm so sorry. Family is important."

Rickie nodded her agreement. She didn't want to get caught up in a discussion about her complicated family history with a woman she barely knew.

"I grew up in foster care," Sandra said. "I didn't have a bad experience. The people were nice, but it wasn't the same as having a loving home and parents. When I met Clay's father, my life finally came together."

It sounded as if Rickie and Sandra had something in common besides Clay, but before she could decide whether to mention their similarities, Margie returned with their drinks—diet soda for Sandra and milk for Rickie.

"So what'll you have for lunch?" Margie asked.

Rickie hadn't even looked at the menu.

"I'll have the chicken salad sandwich on a croissant," Sandra said. "And the fruit cup instead of French fries."

That sounded good. Besides, Rickie had to be back at work before one thirty and didn't want to take the time to ponder the other options. "I'll have the same thing."

When Margie bustled off to take their orders to the kitchen, Sandra continued to speak, surprising Rickie with her candor.

"I loved Clay's father. John and I had a great marriage. But since he was a career military man, we moved around a lot. I would have preferred to stay in one place, but I made a home wherever the Army stationed us— Germany, Washington, Georgia. John's deployments left me lonely, although the other wives were very supportive. We both thought it would be easier if we had children, but after several miscarriages, I brought up the idea of adopting."

Rickie hadn't seen that coming. Had Clay also been adopted? And if so, had he known?

"About the time I first approached an agency, I got pregnant with Clay. He's my miracle baby."

No wonder Sandra adored her son.

"I have to admit," Sandra added, "I doted on that precious little guy. They call women like me helicopter moms these days, but I'd gone through a lot to finally get him in my arms. And when his father died…" She took a deep breath and slowly let it out. She offered

Rickie a warm smile, but a widow's grief still lurked in her eyes. "Well, I didn't want to lose Clay, too. Although that little rascal did everything he could to worry me to death. And if I didn't color my hair, I would have been gray by the time he entered the second grade."

"How did Clay's father die?" Rickie asked.

"In battle. During Operation Desert Storm."

"I'm sorry."

"Me, too. I'll admit that the last thing I wanted Clay to do was to join the military. Sometimes I think he did it to spite me, although I'm proud of him and all he accomplished, both at West Point and in the Army."

"I'm sure you are."

"Then you can probably understand why I'm looking forward to being a grandmother."

Rickie didn't always open up and reveal her past to people, but Sandra was both sweet and kind. Besides, they also seemed to have a lot in common.

"I grew up in foster care, too," Rickie admitted. "So it's really important for me to create a loving home for my children."

Sandra reached across the table and placed her hand over Rickie's. "I have no idea how things will work out between you and my son. Either way, I'd be delighted to do whatever I can to help you create that special home for your babies."

Rickie believed her. And for the first time since she'd lost her parents, she felt as if she might have someone in her corner. "Thank you. I'd appreciate that."

Before either of them could comment, Margie returned with their sandwiches and fruit cups. "Enjoy, ladies."

Rickie had no more than picked up one half of the stuffed croissant when she heard approaching boot steps and the sound of a familiar soft Texas drawl call out, "Hey."

She glanced up to see Clay standing at their table wearing a smile that dimpled his cheeks.

"Mind if I join you?" he asked.

Sandra slid to the side, making room for him to sit in the booth.

"This is a surprise," she said. "I thought you had things to do at home."

"I forgot about my physical therapy appointment, so while I was in town, I thought I'd join you. That is…" He looked across the table at Rickie. "If you don't mind."

"No, not at all." In fact, she was glad he'd shown up. It was in the babies' best interests for her to have a solid relationship with their father and grandmother.

At least, that's what she kept telling herself. But if truth be told, she thought it might be in her best interests, too.

Chapter Eight

Under normal circumstances, Clay never would have intruded upon a private lunch, but he hadn't been able to stay away from this one. Not when he'd been so damn curious about what his mother might be saying to Rickie.

Or what Rickie might tell his mom.

"Well, look who's here!" Margie handed Clay a menu. "I'd heard you got out of the Army and came back to run the Bar M for your grandpa. How's it feel to be home?"

Margie, bless her heart, had better radar than a fighter jet. Too bad her intel wasn't very good. But she wouldn't get squat out of him. Not if she spread it around town that he wasn't happy to be home. Or to be looking at spending the rest of his life ranching.

"It feels good to be moving around without a cane,"

Clay said, hoping to appease her. "But I won't need that menu. I'll have what the sheriff ate."

"You got it."

As Margie walked away, his mother sat back in her seat and smiled at him. "I'm glad you'll be eating a hearty meal for a change."

"I'm really not very hungry, but ordering the special was easier than taking time to read the menu." He glanced across the table at Rickie, who looked especially pretty today with her soft brown curls tumbling over her shoulders. "How's the job going?"

"Great. At least, so far. It's nice being in a clinic again. Only this time I get to work with families instead of soldiers."

"Speaking of clinics and families," his mother said, "do you have an obstetrician?"

"Yes, I do."

"Oh, good. Is the office around here?"

"No, it's in Jeffersville."

Clay wanted to put a halt to the rapid-fire questions, but he cleared his throat instead, reminding his mother of his presence and hoping she'd take the hint. But she didn't.

"Do you have other family and friends living in Jeffersville?" his mother asked.

"No, not really. I only lived there when I was a teenager. After high school, I joined the Army. I've been away six years, and my friends have all moved for one reason or another."

"That's too bad," Mom said, unable to just leave it at that. "Not even a neighbor?"

Clay stiffened. He was tempted to answer for Rickie,

but he bit his tongue. If she wanted to have a relationship with Sandra Masters, she'd have to get used to being quizzed about subjects she might not want to talk about.

"No, I'm afraid not. I had a twin sister, but she died when we were nine."

"Oh, no." His mother reached out and placed her hand around Rickie's shoulder. "I'm so sorry to hear that."

Clay sympathized, too. But unlike his mom, he usually pulled away when things took an emotional turn.

"It was hard when Lainie died," Rickie said, "but I've adjusted. Don't worry about me. I'll be just fine."

Yeah, right. Telling his mother not to worry was like telling a duck to stay out of a pond. But shouldn't someone in his family be emotionally supportive? Someone who'd actually be good at it?

He'd thought so at first, but as he studied the way his mom reached out to Rickie, the way Rickie responded, her honey-brown eyes glistening with tears, he worried that the women might be bonding. And that wasn't what he'd planned to happen today.

Of course, nothing about this situation had been a part of his life plan.

"How long is your temporary job going to last?" Mom asked.

"Two months."

"Why don't you stay with us while you work in Brighton Valley? Our ranch is only a fifteen-minute drive from here, and there's usually no traffic."

"That's really sweet of you," Rickie said. "But I don't want to impose. Besides, I'm trying to fix up the nursery on the weekends. I need a place to bring the babies home to."

Clay was about to mention that he'd promised to paint and to purchase the furniture, which would be his way of telling his mother to back off and not worry about it, but she suddenly brightened.

"I have an idea," Mom said. "Why don't you stay Monday through Thursday nights with us? We have a big house, with lots of room. And then you could drive back to Jeffersville after work on Fridays."

Rickie shot a glance at Clay, her eyes locking in on his as if she was asking his permission. But hell, what was he supposed to say, no? Not when she was looking at him like that and he knew that she didn't have a family.

"We have a guest room with a private bath," he said.

Rickie bit down on her bottom lip, as if giving the invitation a lot of thought. But a beat later, she looked up and smiled. "Sure. Why not?"

Actually, Clay could come up with quite a few reasons why it might not be wise. With Rickie staying on the ranch, it would be difficult for him to maintain his privacy while being supportive from a distance. But then again, she'd only be staying there four nights a week. He could find plenty of things to keep him busy while she was there.

But that didn't seem to be the answer. How busy did he really want to be when she was sleeping just down the hall?

Lunch at Caroline's Diner had gone much better than Rickie had expected it to. She just hoped that she didn't come to regret staying on the Bar M while she worked at the clinic.

"When can we expect you?" Sandra had asked.

Rickie hadn't wanted to rush into anything. And she needed time to pack a few things, so she said, "After I get off work on Monday."

The rest of her first week at the clinic went well, and now it was Saturday morning. She glanced at the clock on the mantel. No, make that early afternoon.

She'd planned to work on the nursery this weekend, which meant picking up everything Clay would need to paint. She wanted to have it here when he showed up, although he hadn't mentioned a time or even which day.

In the meantime, she had another chore to do. Her parents' accountant had called and requested some additional paperwork he needed to complete their last tax return. So she decided to get that out of the way first.

She wasn't entirely sure where to look, but she knew that one of the boxes in the dining room contained their wills and other important papers. So she opened it and began sorting through it. Toward the bottom, she spotted a manila envelope stuffed full. She removed it, then took a moment to straighten and stretch out the crick in her back before carrying it to the table, pulling out a chair and sitting down to go through the contents.

She found several bills that were due about the time of the accident: power, water, cable TV. How had she missed seeing them when she came home from the funeral and began to settle their estate? They'd all been paid, but only after she'd received the past-due notices. So she tossed them to the side, intending to throw them away.

Next she withdrew a white business-size envelope. She didn't think much of it until the return address caught her eye. The Lone Star Adoption Agency had sent it to Mr. and Mrs. Edwin Campbell. It was postmarked six months ago and had already been opened. She flipped open the flap and removed the contents: a handwritten note and a smaller, pink envelope addressed to the agency.

"We received this correspondence addressed to you," someone at the agency had written, "and we are forwarding it to you per our agreement."

The pink envelope they'd included had also been opened. Inside was a handwritten letter on matching stationery. It was addressed to "The Couple Who Adopted Erica Montoya."

My name is Katherine Donahue, although the many children I've fostered over the years, including the Montoya twins, call me Mama Kate. Rickie and Lainie were sweet girls, and I will always remember them fondly. Lainie was frail and in poor health, and Rickie used to look after her as if she were her own child. They had a special bond, and I became especially attached to them. In fact, I had begun the process to adopt them, but before I could do much of anything, I suffered a debilitating stroke. As a result, all the children I'd been fostering had to go to different homes.

It broke my heart to lose those kids, especially Lainie and Rickie. Not a day goes by that I don't think about them, and I continue to pray

*that they're both doing well. From what I under-
stand, Lainie's surgery went better than expected.
The surgeon didn't think she would live through
it, but she surprised him. I'd give anything to be
able to visit both girls, but I'm not able to travel.
In fact, one of the nurses' aides is writing this
letter for me.*

*Last week, a private investigator visited me
here at the convalescent home and asked me if
I had any information on Rickie's adoption. It
wasn't until after he left that I recalled the name
of the agency.*

*I realize you requested a closed adoption, and
I respect that. Children often do better when they
can make a fresh start. However, I would love to
help these two young women reconnect, if you
think Rickie would want to do so I would be delighted to hear from you. I have included my address and phone number. If you decide not to
contact me, I understand.*

*Either way, please give my love to Rickie. I'll
never forget how loving she was to her sister. I'm
so glad she found a forever home.*

Most sincerely yours,
Katherine Donahue

Rickie was stunned. Her sister was alive?

According to Mama Kate's letter, Lainie had faced
a long road to recovery. So she hadn't died in surgery.
And apparently, she'd hired a private investigate to find
Rickie.

Why hadn't her parents mentioned anything about this to her?

Had they intended to? Had the accident happened before they'd gotten a chance to tell her?

Rickie had no idea how long she sat at the dining room table, holding the only connection she had to her sister. It wasn't until the doorbell rang that she finally managed to wrap her mind around the news.

Her brain continued to spin, weaving all kinds of scenarios, as she carried the letter with her. When she opened the door, she found Clay on the stoop.

Apparently, he spotted her rattled expression and sensed something was off.

"What's the matter?" he asked.

"I just got some surprising—and startling—news about my sister." She stepped aside so he could enter. "She didn't die during heart surgery."

"That's good news," he said.

"Yes, but I have no idea where she is. Or how to find her." Rickie led him to the sofa, where they both took a seat.

"Is there any chance she might have moved in with someone in your birth family?" he asked.

"No, our mother passed away when we were babies, and it was all downhill after that. My dad was an alcoholic and couldn't hold down a job. So money was scarce. I can remember nights when he came home late or not at all. Lainie and I had to fend for ourselves. Then, about the time we turned eight, he died in a seedy bar after a drunken brawl, and we were placed in foster care."

Clay took her hand in his and gave her fingers a gentle squeeze. "I don't know what to say. 'I'm sorry' seems so inadequate."

"Thanks, but his death turned out to be a good thing. We were much better off in foster care. At least we got to eat regularly. And that's when my sister's health problems were finally addressed." That was also when the two girls had become separated.

Rickie's adoptive parents had told her that Lainie died during surgery. According to Mama Kate, the doctors hadn't expected her to live. Had her parents lied to her? Or was that merely what they'd concluded had happened?

Now that they were both gone, she'd never know for sure. But they'd always been honest with her. She'd just have to believe they'd heard a rumor and made that assumption.

"Can you get in touch with the agency and see if they have any contact information for your sister?" Clay asked.

"I can try, but the letter doesn't say anything about Lainie being adopted, too." Rickie glanced at the letter she held, then brightened. "Maybe Mama Kate knows something."

"Who's that?"

"Our first foster mom. She's living in a nursing home now, but I have her contact info. I could call her." In fact, she wasn't going to wait another minute.

Rickie carried the letter with her to the kitchen phone, then dialed the number Mama Kate had given.

A woman answered on the second ring. "Shady Oaks Nursing Home. How can I direct your call?"

"I'd like to speak to one of your patients—or residents. Her name is Katherine Donahue."

The woman paused for a beat. "I'm sorry. Katherine passed away last week."

Rickie's soaring heart sputtered and dropped with a thud, reverberating in her ears. This couldn't be happening. If she'd found that letter when she'd first come home…if her parents had mentioned something to her the last time they'd talked…if…

"Ma'am?" the woman on the line said. "Are you still there?"

"Yes. It's just that…" Rickie blew out a sigh. "I'm so very sorry she's gone."

"I'm not sure if this helps, but she passed away peacefully. She told me many times that she was ready."

Yes, but Rickie wasn't ready. Still, she thanked the woman and said goodbye. After the call ended, she turned to find Clay standing behind her. He'd obviously heard her side of the conversation and had connected the dots.

Either that, or he'd seen the tears filling her eyes, because he eased close to her. He didn't say anything, and she was glad that he didn't. Emotion clogged her throat, and she didn't think she would have been able to speak anyway.

As if sensing what she needed, he opened his arms, and she fell into his embrace.

Clay had never been any good when anyone, especially a woman, got weepy. But the minute he'd seen the stricken look on Rickie's face and saw the tears roll down her cheeks, he'd been toast. So he offered the only thing he could think of—a shoulder to cry on.

He wasn't sure how long he held her, her growing belly pressed against him, connecting them in a way, yet holding him at a distance. Still, she clung to him and cried, dampening his shirt. But he wasn't going to complain. Instead, he stroked her back, providing what little support he could, and breathed in the soft scent of her floral shampoo.

She sniffled one last time and drew back, breaking their embrace. Her voice cracked as she said, "I'm sorry to be a crybaby. I'm actually pretty tough, but lately, my hormones do this to me."

He wasn't buying that. She was blaming her tears on her pregnancy, but he knew it was more than an increased level of estrogen at play. Moments earlier she'd believed that she might be able to reunite with the twin she'd thought had died. And that hope had been dashed.

"You don't need to apologize. I understand." And he'd do just about anything to make her feel better, to see her smile again. But at the moment, he didn't have any bright ideas.

She placed her hand on her womb, stroking the swollen mound where her babies grew, and a thought struck. She'd blamed her tears on her pregnancy hormones. Maybe if he appealed to her maternal side, those same hormones might lighten her load and lift her mood.

"I came by to paint the nursery," he reminded her. "Have you chosen the color yet?"

"Yes." She sniffled and used her fingers to wipe the moisture that lingered under her eyes. "I decided on a light green to go with that animal theme. But I haven't bought the paint yet."

"Then let's go get it now. And while we're out, we can look at baby furniture." Spending the entire afternoon with her hadn't been his original plan. In fact, he hated to go shopping, unless it was for groceries, sporting goods or tools. But he'd make an exception today, especially if it made her feel better.

"I can't," she said. "I've probably got red, puffy eyes and a splotchy face. I have no business leaving the house. Just look at me."

He *was* looking at her, and in spite of her casual dress and obvious emotional distress, there was something that appealed to him and caused his heart to swell and his pulse to go wonky. "You look cute. Besides, the redness will go down in a few minutes. And it'll do you good to get out."

"I…I don't know." She combed her fingers through her hair, the luscious locks glossy and soft. She seemed to be on the fence and waffling.

Before he could push a little harder, her eyes opened wide, her lips parted and she let out a silent gasp. Then she reached for his hand and placed it on her abdomen. One of the babies was moving, and he felt a little bump that might be a knee or maybe a butt. It was hard to say, but it was pretty cool.

A big grin stretched across his face. "I feel it."

She held his hand firm. "Wait a minute."

He wasn't going anywhere. Not now. The moment was surreal. Special.

And then it happened. A quick jab to his palm that nearly took his breath away.

* * *

Rickie had no idea if it was their son or daughter who'd given Clay a solid kick, but the moment he felt it, his eyes widened and he broke into a full-on smile. "Wow. That's cool. I've felt foals and calves rumble around in the womb, but never a baby."

"They've been moving a lot lately." She might have been crying just moments ago, but the babies made her laugh now. "It makes me wonder what they're doing in there."

"Does it hurt when they kick like that?"

"No, not at all. I love the way it feels. It makes them seem real."

She lifted her hand off the top of his, but he continued to touch her baby bump as if mesmerized by the experience. She found it pretty amazing, too.

Finally he stepped back and said, "So what do you think? Are you up for a shopping trip?"

"I suppose so."

"Good. Then we can go out to dinner to celebrate."

Her head tilted slightly. "What are we celebrating?"

"Maternal hormones and the miracle of birth." He nodded toward the front door. "Come on. Let's go."

She really wasn't in the mood to shop or to have fun. She'd much rather stay at home and brood about the fact that her sister was alive and that she had no idea how to find her. She'd lost an opportunity to visit Mama Kate, too. It would have been nice to thank the sweet lady for providing her and Lainie with a loving home, even if it had only been temporary.

But Rickie didn't want to hang out at the house alone.

And she actually liked the Clay she'd begun to know. Besides, didn't her babies deserve to have a daddy in their lives?

"All right," she said. "Give me a minute to splash some water on my face and to change clothes."

"Take all the time you need."

She wouldn't take long. Spending the afternoon with the gorgeous father of her twins was beginning to sound like a good idea. It might be too much to hope for, especially when the future never turned out the way she hoped it would, but maybe...if things continued to develop between her and Clay, she'd be able to provide her kids with a loving home, complete with a mommy *and* a daddy.

Chapter Nine

Clay had expected the experience of shopping for baby things to be a real pain in his backside, but so far it hadn't been too bad. He just hoped that when the day was over, and all was said and done, the charges on his credit card were the only costs he'd face.

They first stopped at the hardware store to pick up the paint supplies for the nursery. The last time they'd been there, Rickie had studied the colors carefully, but today she didn't dawdle. She immediately reached for a green swatch and pointed to the lighter shade on the bottom. "This will work perfectly with the comforter set I plan to buy."

He was glad she'd finally chosen the paint for the nursery walls—and relieved that she'd stopped crying. He didn't like seeing her so upset.

After paying for their purchases, Rickie walked beside Clay as he pushed the shopping cart that carried the paint, brushes and other supplies out to his Dodge Ram. Once he unlocked the truck, he placed them in the back seat of the extended cab. Then he drove to a specialty store that sold baby clothes, toys and furniture.

As he followed Rickie up and down the aisles, he couldn't help wondering how much of this stuff the babies really needed. He had a feeling that a lot of the displays were just to tempt new parents into spending more money than they'd budgeted. But what did he really know?

As he'd expected, since it had taken days to choose the paint, Rickie studied the various bedding sets way longer than he thought necessary. After narrowing down the options, she turned to him and asked, "What do you think? If you were a baby, would you rather have your room decorated with jungle animals or cowboys?"

Normally, he'd be inclined to hold back his opinion and let her make the ultimate decision. But in this case, he actually had a preference. It was bad enough that he'd been forced to live a rancher's life. He wasn't about to point his kids in that same direction from the day they were born. So he said, "I like the monkeys."

"Me, too. I was afraid we might have to return the green paint for beige if you preferred the cowboy print."

He didn't mind cowboys. Or ranching, for that matter. It's just that he didn't like being tied to the land, unable to travel to exciting places or pursue his own interests. Of course, now that he was no longer in the Army or able to fly, not much interested him these days.

Rickie put the two comforter sets into the cart, and

then she led him to the furniture section to pick out a chest of drawers, two cribs and mattresses.

"It's a good thing I have a truck," he said.

"Actually, I think we need to order the big items and set up a delivery date." She pointed to a couple of crib styles she liked, then looked up at him. "What do you think?"

His only thought was that her soulful brown eyes had a way of looking into the heart of a man. And Clay didn't like the idea of anyone digging that deep, but she'd asked for his opinion again.

"You choose," he said.

She bit down on her bottom lip, then blew out a soft sigh. "All right, then." She placed her hand on a white, four-in-one convertible model with an arched head-board. "I like this one, but since it's more expensive, I probably ought to go with a simpler style."

He'd brought her shopping to see her happy, so why would he encourage her to get something other than her first choice?

"I prefer that white one, too," he said. "Let's order two of them and get the matching dresser."

Her smile deepened, putting the glimmer back into her eyes, and he looked away, trying to shake the effect her happiness had on him.

"What else do you want to look at?" he asked.

"This will do for now. Once we paint and move in the furniture, that old office will look like a real nursery. Then, on the weekends, I can add other things bit by bit."

"What other things?"

"I'll eventually need a lamp, wall hangings and stuff like that."

The nursery was going to end up costing a boatload of money, and that was before Clay counted baby clothes, diapers, bottles and who knew what else. But he wouldn't complain. He'd expected to take on his share of the financial burden—if not more.

That was about it, though. When it came to babysitting or burping or changing diapers, Rickie would have to look for someone else to step up, because he didn't know squat about babies.

When the kids got old enough, he'd feel more comfortable being around them and doing things with them. He'd teach them to ride a horse, as well as a bike. And he'd take them camping and fishing. But for the first few years, he'd have to leave the entertaining and the day-to-day stuff up to Rickie.

By the time they'd ordered the furniture and set up a delivery date, then packed the comforters in the back seat, on top of the paint supplies, Clay asked Rickie if she was hungry. "If you want, we can stop someplace and get a bite to eat."

"Let's just go home. I'll whip up something for us to eat there."

The day had turned out to be a lot better and more productive than Clay had expected it to. And for some odd reason, going "home" for dinner with Rickie sounded like a nice way to end it.

While Clay prepared the nursery walls for the painting he planned to do another day, Rickie cooked ground turkey then added a jar of marinara to make spaghetti sauce. She also made a green salad. It was an easy and casual meal, but after all Clay had done for her today, she wanted to make it special. So she set the dining room table, using her mother's good china. While tempted, she decided not to light candles, which would provide a romantic vibe. She could hardly look at the hunky rancher without triggering flashbacks of the night they made love, and her memories didn't need any prompts.

While the pasta boiled, she went to the nursery to check on Clay's progress. He'd already washed down the walls and now stood at the window, putting up blue masking tape to protect the glass. He hadn't heard her approach, so she took a moment to admire his work ethic, not to mention his broad shoulders and the way his jeans fit his perfect backside.

As if sensing her presence, he turned to the door and smiled. "Something sure smells good. I'm nearly finished in here for today. I promised my granddad to go with him to purchase a couple more cutting horses tomorrow, so I'll have to come back to finish next Saturday."

"That's not a problem. I'd do it myself, but the fumes aren't good for the twins. I'm just happy to know it'll be done soon."

He placed the roll of tape on the windowsill, crossed his arms and shifted his weight to one hip. "Maybe it would be better if I came back during the week, while you're at work and staying at the ranch. That way, the room can air out and you won't have to deal with the smell."

"That would be great, but…" She couldn't expect him to do that. "It's a long drive."

"I'd have to make the trip no matter which day I paint."

True, but she liked the idea of being home when he came. Besides, once the nursery was painted, he wouldn't have too many reasons to return.

Their gazes locked for a couple of beats, and her heart fluttered the way it had the first time she'd laid eyes on him. It had only been physical attraction then, but he'd been so helpful and supportive today, not to mention incredibly generous, that… Well, she couldn't help thinking that a guy like him would make an awesome father and husband.

Whoa, girl. You're letting those pregnancy hormones run away with you.

Nesting and creating a nursery for the babies was one thing, but imagining Clay in a family scenario was another. She'd better reel in those whacky thoughts before she set herself up for a major disappointment, not to mention heartbreak. She'd already had enough of those to last a lifetime.

She tore her gaze away and nodded toward the door that opened to the hall. "Dinner is just about ready, so you might want to wash up and meet me in the dining room."

"Sounds good."

Ten minutes later, they sat across from each other at the linen-draped table.

"This spaghetti is really good," he said. "But I didn't expect you to work so hard."

"Thank you, but I didn't go to much effort. As far as meals go, this was pretty simple to make."

"Either way, I appreciate it."

She swirled the long pasta strands on her fork only to have them unwind and slide back onto her plate. Too bad she hadn't fixed something that was easier to eat. Next time she'd have to make tacos. That was, if there was a next time.

At least he'd come today. He'd also gone above and beyond, especially when he'd held her in his arms while she'd cried. How many men were that sensitive, that supportive?

Maybe she'd better let him know that she appreciated it. So she said, "I'm sorry for falling apart on you earlier today."

He stopped twirling his fork and looked up. "Don't worry about that. You were hit with both good and bad news at the same time. That's enough to make anyone cry."

Did he ever cry? Somehow she doubted it.

"Are you going to look for your sister?" he asked.

"Yes, but I really don't know where to start."

"You could hire a private investigator."

She set her fork aside and leaned back in her seat. "I think that's what my sister did. Mama Kate said in her letter that a private investigator had contacted her. So my sister might be looking for me."

"Hopefully she'll find you first. But in the meantime, I'll talk to my friend Poncho. He's a cop with the

Wexler Police Department, so I'm sure he can recommend a good PI who's local. He also might have some other ideas and suggestions."

"That would be awesome. I'd give anything to see Lainie again."

"You could also try one of those home DNA kits you get online," Clay said. "People use them to learn about their ancestry, but a lot of them have found lost relatives that way."

"Good idea."

They continued to eat in silence. When they finished, Clay began to clear the table.

Rickie reached for his wrist to stop him. "What are you doing?"

"I'm going to help you clean up."

"Don't be silly. You have a long drive in front of you. Besides, I'll have the dishes washed before you leave city limits."

He offered her a warm, appreciative smile. "Thanks for your concern, but I insist. I'm not going to eat and run."

Since she'd tidied up as she prepared the meal, it didn't take long for them to load the dishwasher.

"See?" he said. "That didn't delay my drive home."

As he headed to the front door, she followed, wondering if he would kiss her good-night. She hoped so, but he'd have to make the first move.

He paused on the stoop and brushed his lips across her forehead, the warmth of his breath lingering on her skin.

"Thanks again for dinner. I'll see you back at the ranch on Monday evening." Then he turned and strode toward his truck, leaving her on the porch with a tingly brow.

She appreciated the friendly gesture, but it was hardly the kind of kiss she'd hoped for. And as he drove away, disappointment settled over her.

What was wrong with her? Clay had been amazing today. He'd shown her a sweet and kind side, and he'd been more than generous. Instead of yearning for more, she ought to be grateful for his support and friendship. Entertaining any thoughts of romance was crazy and would only lead to further disappointment.

Hadn't his mother told her that he hadn't planned to have kids? He probably wasn't marriage minded, either.

Clay might have a playful grin and a soft southern drawl she found mesmerizing, but he'd undoubtedly used it on other women before. He'd certainly charmed her that day on Hawaii's North Shore.

Only trouble was, that same charm had cropped up again today, promising to lure her in once more. And she'd have to be on guard. She couldn't risk another broken heart.

On Monday morning, Rickie packed her things for a four-night stay at the Bar M, then drove to Brighton Valley to start her second workweek. It was business as usual at the family clinic, and before she knew it, five o'clock rolled around.

After the last patient left and Glory locked up, Rickie went out to her car. But instead of driving straight to the ranch, she stopped by a fast food restaurant and picked up something to eat.

She figured Clay's mother would offer to feed her, but she didn't want to make any assumptions or to be any more trouble than necessary. So she headed back onto the highway and munched on a grilled chicken sandwich while she drove.

She'd no more than parked her car by the barn when Sandra stepped out onto the porch and waved in welcome. "Can I help you bring anything into the house?"

"Thanks for the offer, but I've got it." Rickie reached into the back seat and removed her suitcase. Then she crossed the yard and met Sandra on the porch.

"I'm glad you're here. Dinner's almost ready." Sandra opened the door for her and followed her into the house. "We normally eat around five thirty, but Clay and his grandfather went into town for supplies and haven't returned yet. You're probably hungry, so I can get you a snack or appetizer to tide you over."

"Actually, I already had dinner."

"That's too bad. From now on, I hope you'll eat with us on the nights you stay here. It'll be nice to have another woman to talk to. I'm usually stuck with a couple of men who'd rather wolf down their meals than waste their time on conversation."

Rickie laughed. "I was in the Army, remember? I've had plenty of experience with men." She paused as her words sank in. "Oops. That came out wrong. I meant I know all about male habits and mannerisms."

"I knew exactly what you meant." Sandra laughed. "Come on, I'll show you around. Then I'll take you to the guest room so you can get settled."

After a brief tour of the house, Sandra ushered Rickie

into a large, tidy bedroom with a lemony scent. A floral comforter covered a queen-size bed and a green throw rug adorned the hardwood floor.

"You'll have your own bathroom," Sandra said, pointing to an open interior door. "You'll find clean linens on the cupboard. Please make yourself at home. And if there's anything you need, let me know."

"I'll be fine. Thank you."

"Once you unpack," Sandra said, "come to the table. You can have dessert with us. I made a blueberry cheesecake."

Rickie offered her a warm, appreciative smile. "I'll certainly make room for that."

When an engine sounded outside, Sandra brightened. "Clay and Roger, his grandfather, just got home."

Rickie momentarily brightened, too. And her heart skipped a couple beats. But she did her best to quell her excitement and tamp down any romantic thoughts.

"I'd better get dinner on the table," Sandra said. "I hope you'll come and sit with us, even if you're not hungry."

Rickie thanked her but remained in the bedroom even after she unpacked, trying to play it cool. About twenty minutes later, she made her way to the kitchen table, where the small family of three had just finished a meal of meat loaf, baked potatoes and green beans.

Both men stood when she entered. Clay's grandfather, a tall, gray-haired man in his seventies, reached out a big, work-roughened hand in greeting. "I'm Roger Masters. You must be Rickie."

"Yes, sir. It's nice to meet you. Thanks for allowing

me to stay with you on weekday evenings. I'll try not to disrupt your routines or to be a bother."

"Nonsense," Sandra said. "We're happy to have you. And our usual routines could use a little shaking up."

Clay pulled out the chair next to his, and Rickie took a seat. While Sandra cleared the table, the men lapsed into a talk about the new horses they'd just purchased and the ranch foreman's search for another hand.

When Sandra passed out slices of cheesecake, the men quickly dug in, and their conversation stalled.

"Rickie," Sandra said, "how was your day?"

"It was good. I really enjoy working with Dr. Davidson."

"Any exciting moments?"

"Actually, two. A woman came in for a checkup, and while she was sitting on the exam table, she mentioned having an upset stomach and an ache in her jaw. It turned out that she was having a heart attack. We'd no more than sent her off in an ambulance to the hospital when a mother brought in a kid who'd sliced a deep cut in his knee while trying to saw into a watermelon with a bread knife."

"How in the hell did he do that?" Roger asked.

Rickie'd wondered the same thing when she'd first talked with him and his mom. "Apparently, he was sitting on the floor and holding the melon in his lap."

The elderly rancher chuckled and shook his gray head. "That boy's lucky he only sliced into his knee."

At that, Rickie laughed.

"When is your next doctor's appointment?" Sandra asked.

"It's on Friday afternoon." Rickie glanced at Clay. "A lot of fathers go to those appointments. Let me know if that's ever something you might like to do. You'd be able to see the babies on the ultrasound."

She'd expected him to decline, but he surprised her when he said, "Sure. Why not? I'll pick you up at the clinic. That way we won't end up with two cars in Jeffersville."

Stunned by his response, Rickie was still reeling when Sandra said, "I'd like to go, too."

Before Rickie could tell her she was more than welcome, she caught a frown on Clay's face and bit her tongue. Didn't he want his mom to go with them?

Clay's mother was getting way too involved. Fortunately, when he cut her a stern glance, she took the hint.

"I didn't mean to suggest that I tag along to that appointment," she said. "But I'd love to go to another one with you someday."

"Of course," Rickie said. "I'm going to schedule my appointments as late in the afternoon as possible so I don't have to miss too much work."

"Maybe we can make an evening of it," Mom said, apparently forgetting Clay's silent admonishment. "The men can call out for pizza or something, and we can have dinner in Jeffersville. We can even go shopping. You're going to need a lot of baby things, and the twins will be here before you know it."

"Clay already bought the major stuff," Rickie said. "So I have the cribs, mattresses and bedding."

"That still leaves plenty of other things to buy. And

I'd love to shop for baby clothes with you." Suddenly his mother brightened. "I have an idea. I can plan a shower. I have a lot of friends from church and the Wexler Women's Club who'd come."

Clay didn't doubt it. Sandra Masters was the friendly type with a big heart and a generous nature. So women seemed to gravitate to her. She was also easy for them to talk to, so they often confided in her and asked for advice.

That's why it frustrated her that Clay kept his thoughts and feelings under lock and key. It didn't help that Granddad was pretty tight-lipped about his feelings, too.

Yet Rickie seemed to open right up. Clay had expected the two of them to hit it off, but they were getting a little too chummy for his comfort. As they talked about invitations, possible dates and the guest list, Clay stiffened.

As if sensing the tension in the room, Granddad chimed in, as usual, in an attempt to defuse it. "I picked up a DVD of that new Denzel Washington flick while I was out. Anyone else up for a movie?"

"I am," Rickie said. "I love his movies."

"Good. Come on. I'm going to put it on in the den."

As Granddad got to his feet, Rickie began to clear the table of the dessert plates and forks, but Clay stopped her. "Oh, no, you don't. I have cleanup duty tonight."

Once Rickie left the kitchen and was out of hearing range, Clay approached his mother, who stood at the sink.

"Slow down, Mom. You're moving way too fast."

Her brow furrowed. "I'm sorry, honey. I didn't mean to overstep. It's just that..." She paused and blew out a ragged sigh. "I like Rickie. And she's all alone. I only want to help."

"I get that. But it's not your job to mother her. I'm still trying to wrap my brain around all that's happening to me. And I feel..." He paused. Hell, he knew exactly how he felt. Scared. Backed into a corner. But there was no way he'd readily admit it, especially to a woman who'd dedicated her life to fixing things.

His mother placed her hand on his cheek, her gaze loving. "I know it's a little scary for you, especially because you never really knew your father and you didn't grow up with younger brothers and sisters. But believe me when I say this. You're going to love those babies the moment you see them. And you're going to be an amazing dad."

Clay hoped she was right. Because, quite frankly, he had his doubts.

Chapter Ten

Clay drove to Rickie's house in Jeffersville twice the following week. The first time was on Monday morning, after he'd gone to physical therapy. She'd given him her key so he could go inside and paint the nursery. He'd stayed long enough to get the job done, clean up afterward and air things out. Hopefully, she wouldn't have any fumes to contend with when she returned to the house after the end of her workweek.

He'd made that second drive today so that someone would be home when the baby furniture arrived. After the deliverymen left, Clay put both cribs together and set them in the spots Rickie had pointed out when she'd told him of her plans to convert the office into a nursery.

He probably should have locked up the house at that point, but he opened one of the comforter sets so he could get an idea of what the room was going to look like after Rickie made the final touches on the project. Then he'd folded the bedding again and put it back into the plastic pouch.

He had a feeling she was really going to be happy when she saw it. And oddly enough, that made him happy, too.

As it turned out, her doctor's appointment was today. He'd made plans to meet her at the obstetrician's office, which meant he had to hang around in Jeffersville for an hour or so. But he didn't mind. He took the opportunity to explore the area, particularly the main drag, which was within walking distance of Rickie's house.

There he spotted a drugstore, a small post office, a mom-and-pop market and even a fast food restaurant with a drive-through window—Bubba's Burger Barn.

Jeffersville wasn't nearly as big and spread out as Wexler. Nor was it as quaint and touristy as Brighton Valley. But as far as small Texas communities went, it was probably an okay place to live.

The only downside was the distance Clay would have to drive from the Bar M whenever he wanted to visit Rickie and the kids, but he'd get used to it. His truck had a good CD player, so he could listen to his favorite music or to books on tape.

He glanced at the clock on the dash and decided it was time to head over to the doctor's office, but before he could turn off the main drag, his cell phone rang. Poncho's number flashed on the lit display, which was a relief. Clay had called him last Saturday night and had left a voice mail message, but he hadn't heard from the guy in nearly a week.

"Dude," Clay said. "Where the heck have you been? I thought I might have missed seeing a ransom note."

"Sorry about that. I took a week's vacation and spent it fishing at a lake in Canada with a couple of guys from my gym. The cell reception was terrible up there, so I didn't get your message until I got home. What's up?"

"A lot." So much, in fact, that Clay wasn't sure where to start. He began by telling Poncho about Rickie's surprise visit to the ranch and the news of her pregnancy.

"Oh, wow. *Twins?* Are you sure she's telling you the truth?"

Clay'd had his doubts at first, but he'd come to the conclusion that they had to be. There hadn't been any reason for Rickie to lie to him. "Yeah," he said, "I'm sure."

"How do you feel about it?"

"Uneasy. A little scared." Clay didn't open up to just anyone, but Poncho had always been safe—and a good sounding board. "At times, I feel like I'm in over my head, but I'm going to do the right thing."

"You mean you're going to *marry* her?"

"Slow down. I wouldn't go that far. Marriage wouldn't just ground me, it'd probably put me six feet under."

Poncho seemed to chew on that for a moment. "You two hit it off pretty good on the beach."

"That's for sure."

"Has that changed?"

"No, not really." Clay found Rickie just as attractive as ever, just as appealing. But more than that, he'd come to see that she had a good heart. A tender one. And at times he felt compelled to wrap her in his arms. Not just to make love with her, but to protect her. She seemed vulnerable these days, no matter how much she insisted she didn't need any help.

"So why do I sense there's a problem?"

"I guess there isn't one." Other than Clay's fear of being a hands-on father, of failing his children. But Poncho, of all guys, ought to understand that.

In spite of his reluctance to share his feelings, particularly his lack of confidence, Clay said, "Hell, I pretty much grew up without a dad. So what do I know about being a father?"

"I didn't have one, either," Poncho said. "But you know what it's like to be a kid."

"Yeah, I guess so." But Clay didn't remember being a baby. Nor did he know much about them or their needs—other than the fact that they were fragile and needed lots of love and attention.

They cried a lot, too. And it seemed the only things that made them happy or content were rocking chairs, bottles, and kisses and hugs. Just the thought of getting involved with all of that, of being unable to become emotionally attached to them, was enough to convince Clay to stay out of Rickie's way until the twins were old enough to go to school.

The two men grew silent, and Clay continued the drive to the obstetrician's office, following the directions he'd been given. As he pulled into the parking lot, he added, "For what it's worth, I think Rickie will be a great mother."

"That ought to be a relief."

"Yeah, it's huge." Clay parked in an open space and shut off the ignition, but he remained seated behind the wheel.

"So what *aren't* you telling me?" Poncho asked.

"I don't know. I really like her, but I can't give her what she needs."

"You realize that means another man will probably end up raising your kids someday."

"I realize that. And I'm not sure that I like the idea. Know what I mean?"

"Yeah, I do. I had a stepfather, remember? And it was no secret that he didn't like having me around."

Clay remembered some of the stuff Poncho had told him when they were kids and blew out a sigh.

"There are other options," Poncho said. "You don't have to make a marital commitment. You could live together. Or you could just be lovers."

"I don't think Rickie would go for something like that. Family is really important to her—more than most women, I think. And I'm not a family sort of guy." Rather than delve too deep into the touchy-feely stuff, Clay changed the subject to his reason for calling Poncho in the first place. "Speaking of family, Rickie and her twin sister were separated as kids, and she'd really like to find her. Can you recommend a good private investigator?"

"Actually, I can. Once I get back to the precinct, I'll give you his contact info."

"Thanks. I'd appreciate that."

Poncho paused for a moment. "By the way, I just heard that one of the Life Flight pilots is moving out of state after the first of the year. Any chance you'd be interested in taking his job?"

Hell, yes. In a heartbeat. "I wish I could, but I'm afraid I won't be able to pass the required eye exam."

"That's too bad."

To say the least.

"Listen," Poncho said, "I have to go. I'll give you a call later with the investigator's contact number. In the meantime, check your calendar. It's time for another poker night. If we're lucky and Duck isn't on the rodeo circuit, maybe he'll be able to join us."

"Sounds good. I'll bring the beer."

After the call ended, Clay left his truck in the parking lot and entered the doctor's office. He scanned the waiting room and spotted Rickie sitting in a chair near the window, thumbing through a parenting magazine. She wore a pair of black slacks and a light blue shirt that molded her baby bump. As she stopped turning pages and zeroed in on an article she must have found interesting, her dark curls tumbled over her shoulders.

She looked…cute. And maternal. Yet at the same time, he found her as sexy as hell.

He took a moment longer to admire her then crossed the room and took the seat next to her. "Sorry I'm late."

She looked up and smiled, those honey-brown eyes having a sweet effect on him. "No problem. I thought something might have come up. Or else you changed your mind."

Before he could respond, a brunette dressed in pink scrubs and holding a medical file opened the door and called, "Erica Campbell."

"Come on." Rickie set the magazine aside, got to her feet and reached for her purse. "This is it."

So it was. Clay had flown night ops in dangerous situations without blinking an eye, but he'd never been in a situation like this, one that tickled his nerves to the point of sweaty-palmed apprehension.

His heart was thudding so hard he could feel it in his ears. He imagined those thumps as a warning in Morse code. *Watch out. Do not get sucked in over your head.*

But as he followed the nurse and Rickie into the farthest part of the back office, he wiped his hands on his denim-clad thighs and pushed through it.

Rickie lay on the exam table, her belly exposed, while Dr. Raquel Gomez applied the gel. Each time she had the opportunity to see the twins on the ultrasound screen, excitement soared. But today, she focused on Clay. He appeared a bit pale and wide-eyed, reminding her of a possum in the headlights.

"This is going to be cool," she told him. "There's nothing to be nervous about."

"I'm not nervous." A twitch in his eyes mocked his words, and she couldn't help but smile.

"Dad," Dr. Gomez said, "you'll get a better view if you step around to the right side of the table."

Rickie wasn't sure Clay actually wanted to get a good look. But he did as he was told.

"Here we go," the doctor said as she moved the probe over Rickie's belly. "There's Baby A."

"That's the girl," Rickie told Clay, whose nervous expression had morphed into one of awe.

Thank goodness. Rickie always found it heartwarming to see her son and daughter moving around inside her womb, but she'd been worried that Clay might find it overwhelming.

"That's amazing," he said. "Just look at her." He leaned forward and studied the screen. "Is she sucking her thumb?"

"She certainly is." Dr. Gomez continued to scan the baby, taking time to make measurements. "And she's growing nicely. She's measuring at twenty-one weeks and three days, which is a little small, but that's to be expected with multiples."

Rickie had known the twins were getting bigger. Her waistline certainly was. And their movements had gotten stronger.

"Here's Baby B," the doctor said. "And he's right on target, too. He's measuring twenty-two weeks, one day."

The doctor took a few more measurements. When the scan was complete, she wiped the gel from Rickie's belly and gave her a towelette to use to clean up. Then she helped her sit up.

As Rickie adjusted her shirt, the doctor said, "Both babies look good. The placentas are healthy, the heartbeats are strong. And they're growing at a steady rate. Do you have any questions?"

"Not that I can think of." Rickie glanced at Clay. "Do you?"

"No, not really."

"Then I'll see you in three weeks." Dr. Gomez reached out and shook Clay's hand. "It's always nice to have the fathers come in for these appointments." Then she left them alone.

"So what did you think?" Rickie asked Clay.

"I'm stunned. This makes them seem…real."

She'd felt the same way the first time she'd seen them on the ultrasound, their little hearts beating like crazy. And now, when they tumbled around and kicked inside, there was no doubt. Not only were they real, but she'd be holding them in her arms one day soon.

As Rickie got off the exam table and stepped onto the floor, Clay asked, "Have you decided on their names?"

"No, not really. I was going to name the girl after my sister. But now that I have reason to believe Lainie's alive and that I might find her someday, I'd better come up with something else." Maybe Katherine, she thought, after Mama Kate. "I'll think of something."

Clay nodded his agreement. "What about the boy?"

"I'm not sure. I like David."

"Maybe you should consider calling him Goliath instead, since he's so much bigger than his sister?"

Rickie laughed. "Very funny."

He shrugged, then said, "It's up to you. But if I had a say in naming them, I'd call the boy Jonathon—after my dad."

"I like that." She also liked the idea that Clay had laid claim to the twins, which seemed like a sure sign that he'd be involved in their lives. "And just so you know, you do have a say about things."

Hopefully, she wouldn't regret telling him that. Up until two weeks ago, Clay hadn't known anything about her pregnancy. And while there were times, especially in the beginning, when she'd felt all alone, adrift on an uncharted sea, she'd also been able to make all the decisions on her own, without any outside interference.

As they left the exam room, Clay said, "I'm going to drive through Bubba's Burger Barn and pick up dinner. Then I'll meet you at home."

Home. Coming from Clay, in his soft Texas drawl, the word had a nice ring to it, reminding her of the family she'd hoped to create, complete with two children, a mommy *and* a daddy.

While Rickie waited at the reception desk to make her next appointment, Clay headed for the clinic door. She studied the former Black Hawk commander as he walked with assurance, admiring the broad shoulders that suggested he could carry a heavy load—be it physical or emotional—as well as the denim-clad hips and the sexy swagger that reminded her he knew how to treat a woman.

If things continued to progress like they had over the past two weeks, if the two of them grew closer, maybe they'd become lovers again. If so, then her children would not only have a loving father, but she'd have a special man in her life. A friend and helpmate who'd stick by her through thick and thin, who'd love her in sickness and in health. For richer, for poorer.

She'd had plenty of disappointments over the years and suffered more than her share of losses. She didn't want to jinx anything at this stage of the game, but if her intuition proved true, her luck had finally changed.

On the way home from the doctor's office, Rickie stopped to get gas. By the time she'd parked in her driveway and shut off the ignition, Clay's truck had pulled up along the curb. When he got out, he carried a white paper bag holding their food and a drink carrier with two disposable cups.

She didn't usually eat beef or French fries, but the food would be filling, and the cleanup was going to be a breeze. She would have preferred a more romantic dinner, but Clay's heart had been in the right place, and his offer to pick up their meal was both thoughtful and sweet.

After unlocking the front door and letting them inside, Rickie caught a whiff of fresh paint, but the odor wasn't very strong.

Clay set the bag and drinks on the dining room table, then tossed her a boyish grin. "Come on. I can't wait for you to see how the room looks."

She followed him down the hall. When she entered her father's old office, she scanned the green walls, the white cribs, the cute jungle-print bedding, still in the plastic bags and even cuter at home than in the stores.

"This is amazing," she said. "I can't believe the transformation. The nursery looks better than I'd hoped it would."

She turned to Clay, who stood close to her side, watching her reaction to all he'd accomplished. A sense of pride lit his eyes, and her heart took a tumble. "I don't know how to thank you."

Without a conscious thought, she wrapped her arms around him and gave him an appreciative hug. But the moment she felt the warmth of his arms and breathed in his musky, mountain-fresh scent, memories of the slow dance in the sand filled her head, reminding her of the chemistry they had the night they'd made love.

Was he having flashbacks, too?

She drew back just enough to look into his heated gaze. She felt compelled to draw his mouth to hers, but he beat her to it and kissed her as if this evening was just a continuation of that first night.

She relished his taste, his skilled tongue, and leaned into him. But before she could lose herself in him, he drew back and removed his lips from hers.

"I'm sorry," he said. "I didn't mean to overstep."

"You didn't."

He glanced at her baby bump, yet kept his thoughts to himself.

"I'm sorry," she said. "I'm afraid my belly is a lot bigger than it used to be." She hoped it wasn't a turnoff.

"I don't care about that. It's just that I don't want to hurt you."

"You won't. Pregnant women have sex all the time." Her cheeks warmed. "I mean, that's what I read. I haven't actually…" She paused, trying to regroup, and her cheeks warmed. After all, he'd only kissed her. He hadn't said a thing about doing any more than that.

Apparently, he knew what she'd been trying to explain, because he pulled her back into his arms and kissed her again, his tongue seeking hers. As his hands roamed along the curve of her back, passion built to the boiling point, and at the same time, so did her hopes and dreams.

Whatever this was, whatever they'd shared in the

past, was more than chemistry, more than sex. At least, it meant a lot more than that to her.

Again, Clay paused and took a half step back. His gaze caressed her, a loving touch she felt as strongly as if he'd done it with his hands. "You're beautiful, Rickie—inside and out."

She was both flattered and skeptical at the same time. As a result, she let out an awkward little chuckle. "I not only look like a blimp, I feel like one, too."

He placed his hand on her swollen womb in a way that seemed almost reverent. "Seeing you like this, with the babies growing inside, makes you all the prettier. And all the more appealing."

His sweet words and his gentle touch stroked something deep in her heart and soul, and she knew at that very moment that she could love this man.

Who was she kidding? She'd already fallen in love with him.

They stood like that for a moment, lost in an unexpected reality. Then she reached for his hand and led him to her bed, where he kissed her again, stirring up a rush of feelings, both physical and emotional.

As they slowly removed their clothing, Rickie knew that this night would be special—and more memorable than the last. They'd reached a turning point to their budding relationship, and it would only get better from here.

She pulled back the coverlet, and they moved to the bed, where they kissed again. Their hands seemed to remember all the right places to touch, to caress. Tongues mated, breaths mingled and hands stroked until she thought she might die if they didn't make love.

Clay hovered over her, and she reached for his erection and guided him right where she wanted him to be, to come. *Home*.

He entered her slowly, taking time to consider the babies, to be gentle. But it was nearly impossible for her to hold back. As her body responded to his, harmonizing in a loving tune only the two of them could hear, she reached a peak, arched her back and let go.

He shuddered, releasing with her in a sexual explosion that would have lit up the night sky if they'd been outside, shattering stars and filling the air with a silent profession of love and forever.

She felt compelled to say it out loud, to tell him exactly how she felt. Instead, she held back, savoring the moment and envisioning their future together. Together, they'd create a perfect home, plan family holidays and spend each night like this, wrapped in each other's arms.

Surely he was having those same thoughts…

Clay lay still, caught up in an amazing afterglow. He hadn't expected to make love with Rickie tonight, although, given their off-the-charts chemistry, he couldn't say that he was surprised. It's just that he had no idea where to go from here. The renewed intimacy between them would make it difficult for him to maintain a safe emotional distance, but did that matter?

He had to admit that their bodies were in tune with each other, and that the sex had been even better tonight than before. But she was probably going to expect some kind of commitment from him, which would be life altering. And his life had changed enough already.

Still, they couldn't go on as if nothing had happened. Could they?

Poncho had suggested that they could become lovers without moving in together or making any serious promises, but Clay couldn't suggest something like that now. Not when he wasn't sure how he felt about all that was happening. Hell, he wasn't sure how he felt about anything.

"Are you hungry?" Rickie asked, pressing a kiss to his shoulder. "We could eat those burgers. They're probably cold, but I can warm them up."

Actually, Clay would prefer to pass on dinner altogether. He needed time to wrap his mind around what they'd just done—and what it might mean.

"I know that I was the one to suggest we eat together, but now that we…" He glanced at her, still wrapped in his arms, and forced a smile. "Well, we got a little sidetracked. Would you mind if I took a burger to go?"

"No, that's fine. What's going on?"

Nothing, actually. He just needed some time alone, time to think and sort things through. But he'd have to come up with a believable excuse, and one that wasn't an out-and-out lie. "My grandfather and I have an early day planned, which means it'll start before dawn. And I have to stop at a neighboring ranch to pick up a few things beforehand, so I really need to go."

"Okay. I understand." She offered up a smile, but it seemed a little…uneasy.

Damn. He didn't mean to stress her out. He just

needed some space so he could figure out how he felt about her. About *this*.

He stroked her cheek, then kissed her brow. "I'll see you on Monday evening."

"All right."

He got out of bed, picked up his discarded clothing and got dressed, taking his time so he didn't appear to be eager to escape. The excuse he'd given her seemed to be working, but he didn't feel too good about it.

Rickie stepped out of bed, pulled a robe out of her closet and slipped into it. She tied the sash under her breasts, which emphasized her baby bump.

The sight intrigued him, yet scared him, too.

It might help if he knew he wasn't leaving her high and dry.

"Are you okay with…?" He nodded toward the bed, the sheets rumpled from where they once lay. "With what we just did?"

She smiled. "Yes, but it would be nice if you could stay longer. And spend the night."

"Maybe next time." But would there even be a next time? He wasn't sure.

Rickie followed him out to the living room. The house was quiet, other than the sound coming from the antique clock on the mantel, its second hand clicking a steady cadence. With each tick-tock, Clay's uneasiness rose.

He'd done his best to avoid love and family in the past. He'd always blamed his philosophy on the need to be a man and a war hero like his father. That's also why he'd resisted his mother's attempts to smother him and keep him under her wing. He'd also done his best to keep her at an emotional distance. But now he wasn't so sure about anything.

There was something nice to be said about having Rickie in his life. He had feelings for her.

Could it be love? He wasn't sure. If it was, he had no idea what to do about it.

Once he reached the front door, he gave Rickie a kiss goodbye. Then he headed for his pickup, both glad to be on the road and a bit hesitant about leaving.

It had been an interesting day, to say the least, and as he pulled out onto the highway, he was still reeling from all that had transpired. And that feeling didn't ease until long after he got home.

Even then, when he'd gone to bed for the night, he still hadn't come up with a suitable answer to his dilemma—other than he needed time to sort it out.

More than once, he felt the urge to reach for his cell, to apologize for leaving so quickly. But then what?

That would only lock him into a relationship that scared the crap out of him. For that reason, he decided not to talk to Rickie again until she arrived at the ranch on Monday night.

He just hoped he'd have it all figured out by then.

Chapter Eleven

Rickie wished Clay had spent the night with her, but she understood why he couldn't. He had responsibilities and commitments, and he took them seriously. That was just one more reason why she'd fallen in love with him.

"Maybe next time," he'd said.

She wasn't sure why he'd used the word *maybe*. Probably because it would be up to her to extend the invitation. And, of course, she would. Hopefully, she'd have that opportunity soon, because she couldn't wait until they would be together again.

The next morning, she woke early, glad that it was Saturday and eager to get a few household chores done so she could begin decorating the nursery.

She fixed a bowl of cereal for breakfast and set it on the counter, where she intended to eat. She'd no more than poured a glass of orange juice to go with it when her cell phone dinged, indicating an incoming text.

When she glanced at the screen and spotted Clay's number, her heart swelled. She quickly she clicked on the message box to see what he had to say and read, Poncho sent me the contact info for a PI, so I'm forwarding it. Hopefully he can help you find Lainie. If you mention his name, he knows Poncho as Detective Adam Santiago.

The investigator was with a firm located in Wexler. And his name was Darren Fremont.

Rickie looked at the clock on the microwave. It was probably too early to call, but she decided to do it anyway. Worst case, she'd be able to leave a voice mail message.

As luck would have it, the phone was answered on the second ring. "Langley Investigative Services. This is Darren Fremont."

After introducing herself and telling the man who'd referred her, Rickie explained the reason for her call.

"My sister's name is Elena Montoya. We were both in foster care until we were nine, when she had open-heart surgery. I'd been told she hadn't lived through it, but I've just learned that wasn't the case. As far as I know, she stayed in the system. Either way, I haven't seen her since."

"I'll need as much information as you can give me," the PI said. "For starters, give me the name of the last school she attended and the county where you lived back then. I'll start there and see what I can do."

Rickie told him everything she remembered, going

back as far as when their father had custody. "I don't remember the exact date he died, but it happened during a bar fight. I'm sure it made the local news."

"I've got a big case coming up at the end of the week," Darren said, "and that'll keep me pretty busy. But finding your sister shouldn't be too difficult."

Rickie hoped he was right. And that her sister hadn't been adopted in a closed adoption, like she'd been. Not only would it be more difficult to find her, she'd probably have a new last name. They discussed the payment, which included a hundred-dollar-per-hour fee, as well as all expenses.

"That's not a problem." Rickie didn't care about the cost. She'd mortgage the house to the hilt if that's what it took to find her twin.

"I'll be in touch," Darren said.

Rickie thanked him, then ended the call. For the first time in ages, her life was finally coming together and the future looked bright and full of promise.

Hopefully Darren Fremont was as good at finding people as Poncho—or rather, Detective Santiago—said he was. If that were the case and Rickie's luck held out, the sisters could be reunited within days.

On Monday afternoon, Clay drove into town to pick up supplies. Rather than rushing home for dinner, when Rickie would be there, he found himself dragging his feet and looking for various reasons to stay away.

He realized that he and Rickie would eventually talk about Friday night and what it might or might not mean in the future, but he wasn't ready to discuss it yet. Not when he still wasn't sure how he felt about it. A part of him liked the idea of taking their relationship to a deeper level, yet another part was afraid of what she might expect from him.

By the time he arrived home and entered the house through the mudroom, he heard his mom and Rickie chatting in the kitchen.

"Clay," his mom said. "You're finally home. I put your dinner on the stove to keep it warm."

"Thanks." After washing up in the mudroom sink, he proceeded to the kitchen and found his plate on the table, across from where Rickie sat.

She looked especially nice tonight in a white blouse and dark slacks, and she blessed him with a smile. He did his best to return it, then took a seat. As he began to eat, the women lapsed back into the conversation they'd been having.

"Did the investigator say how long he thought it would take to find Lainie?" his mother asked.

"Not exactly. He said it shouldn't be too hard. I got the feeling I might hear something from him by the end of the week."

"That's great news. I'm so happy for you, Rickie."

Clay continued to eat as the women went on to talk about the importance of family. He couldn't argue with that. But what caused him some concern was the way his mother had warmed up to Rickie. The two of them seemed to have grown awfully close in a very short period of time. But then, his mom had always wanted more children, especially a daughter. And she'd made it pretty clear that she was determined to have a relationship with the twins.

By the time Clay carried his plate to the sink, the two women had moved on to baby talk.

"I'd love to schedule that shower within the next two weeks," his mom said. "I've already bought the invitations, but I think we should wait to set a date until you hear something from the private investigator. That way, we can make sure your sister is able to attend."

"That would be awesome, Sandra."

"I think so, too. Fingers crossed." Mom scooted her chair away from the table and got to her feet. "Let's have a bowl of ice cream to celebrate."

"I'm pretty full after that delicious meal," Rickie said.

"Try to make room." Mom winked. "The calcium will be good for the babies."

Rickie laughed. "Good point."

Clay blew out a sigh. His mother was certainly doting on Rickie. Not that there was anything wrong with that. But it was easy to see that she was going to be a helicopter granny.

Mom pulled three bowls out of the cupboard, then turned to Clay. "I'll dish up a large helping for you, too, son. I know how much you like ice cream."

Damn, Clay thought. He was getting sucked into the female chatter, which made him want to bolt. So on principle alone, he said, "I'll pass on dessert tonight."

"Suit yourself." She dished up two bowls then handed one to Rickie.

Before he could rinse his plate and put it in the dishwasher, his mother brought up Thanksgiving. "I hope you'll join us here on the ranch."

"Thank you, Sandra. I'd love to."

Clay supposed it was only natural to include Rickie. Where else would she go?

"I know it's still three weeks away," Mom added, "but it's not too soon to plan the menu."

"I have my mother's recipe book, so I can bring candied yams. Or maybe a pie."

"That sounds good, but don't bother making it at home. It'll be fun to cook and bake together."

When Rickie's face brightened, Clay's shoulders tensed. He didn't mind having Rickie spend the holiday with them or helping his mom cook. But it seemed to be a foregone conclusion that he and Rickie had become a couple.

After they'd made love on Friday, Rickie seemed to have made that jump, too. Not that Clay was completely opposed, but he didn't want to be pushed.

Or rushed.

Unlike his mom, he didn't rush heart first into anything. Life was simpler that way. And safer.

Before Clay could excuse himself and escape to his bedroom, Rickie's cell phone rang. She reached for it, glanced at the lighted display and gasped. "Oh my gosh. It's Darren Fremont."

The investigator? Clay decided to stay put, although he doubted the man had uncovered any news yet. He might only have a question or two for Rickie.

Clay couldn't hear what the guy had to say, but he

was able to watch Rickie's expression and hear her side of the conversation.

Rickie's eyes grew wide, and she tightened her grip on the phone. "That's amazing. Where is she?"

She listened for a while, then asked, "Where is that?"

A couple of beats later, she said, "Just a minute." Then she looked at Clay's mother. "Sandra, can you please get me a pen and paper?"

His mom jumped right on it. She hurried to open a kitchen drawer, pulled out a pad and pencil then handed them to her. Moments later, Rickie took note of something the investigator said.

Clay continued to listen as Rickie made several oohs and aahs.

"I can't tell you how much I appreciate this, Darren. How much do I owe you?" Rickie glanced at Clay and grinned. "He did, huh? That was very sweet of him."

Clay shrugged. He'd told Poncho to tell the PI that he'd take care of expenses. At the time, he'd wanted to see Rickie happy. Hell, he still did. But he also had another motive. If her sister came around, that meant she wouldn't need him or his mother to be her support system, right? At least, that's what he'd told himself.

Once Rickie ended the call, she burst into a bubbly laugh, and her eyes glistened with unshed tears. The happy variety, he assumed.

"Lainie is definitely alive and doing well. In fact, she's married now, and her new husband hired a different PI to look for me. But because of the closed adoption, he ran into a dead end."

"So where is your sister now?" Mom asked. "Do you have a phone number?"

"She and her husband are on a Disney cruise with their three little boys. Can you believe it? She has her own family now."

"Goodness," Mom said. "She's been awfully busy. Did she have triplets?"

Rickie laughed. "I don't have too many details, but according to the PI, Lainie and her husband met while she worked at a ranch. The two of them took in three young brothers as foster kids. Then once they got married, they proceeded to adopt them. It was final last week, so they took the kids on that cruise to celebrate."

"She sounds like a wonderful, loving woman," Mom said. "I like her already and can't wait to meet her. When will she get back?"

"I don't know. About a week. So I'll have to wait to talk to her after she gets home."

"Where's home?" Clay asked.

"In Brighton Valley. Can you believe it? She's not too far from here. And neither is the place where she used to live. It's a home for retired cowboys called the Rocking Chair Ranch, and she still spends a lot of time there. Do you know where it is?"

"I've heard of it," Clay said. "My buddy Matt, the guy we call Duck, rides bulls on the circuit. The last time I talked to him, he mentioned that he's going to take part in the Rocking Chair Rodeo, a local event that will promote the ranch, as well as a group home for abused and neglected children."

"This is amazing," Rickie said. "My sister has done

pretty well for herself—a husband and a family. That's all she and I ever wanted when we were kids. Well, that and being together."

"I know how you feel." His mother gave Rickie an affectionate hug. "I'm so happy for you."

Actually, so was Clay. And he was glad he'd played a small part in it.

Rickie stepped away from his mom, her eyes sparkling. "You know what? I think I'll drive out to that ranch tomorrow after I finish working at the clinic. My sister won't be there, but at least I can see a place that's important to her. And I can meet some of the people she cares about. That will make me feel close to her."

For some reason, that made sense to Clay. Rickie had believed that her twin sister had died sixteen years ago. And now that she'd learned the truth, she had to be eager to reconnect.

And wasn't that good news for him?

"A home for retired cowboys sounds like a really cool place," Rickie said. "I'm looking forward to seeing it."

Actually, Clay had thought the idea was pretty cool when Duck had mentioned it. "I'll tell you what. I'll meet you at the clinic. Then we can drive together so you don't have to go on your own."

Those glistening, honey-brown eyes and that bright smile damn near turned him inside out.

"You'd do that for me?" she asked.

"Yeah." He'd actually been doing a lot for her in the past two weeks. He wasn't the least bit sorry, but he wished he knew why he felt compelled to keep offering.

Just minutes ago he'd convinced himself to take a step back. But for some crazy reason, he'd done the opposite once again.

He hoped he hadn't unwittingly stepped into a mire of emotional quicksand, but it was too late to backpedal now.

True to his word, Clay showed up at the clinic at twenty minutes after four. Rickie had already asked if she could take off a half hour early, and Glory had agreed.

"Are you ready to go?" he asked.

"Yes, but will you come with me for a minute?"

"Sure."

She led him to the back office so she could introduce him to her boss. Moments later, she found Glory seated at the desk in her office. "Dr. Davidson, this is my…friend Clay Masters."

Clay extended his hand in greeting. "It's nice to meet you, Doctor. Rickie speaks highly of you."

The doctor took Clay's hand and smiled. "Please, call me Glory. I've heard some nice things about you, too."

They made small talk for a moment or two. Then Rickie said, "If we want to get to the ranch before the dinner hour, we'd better go."

Five minutes later, they'd climbed into Clay's pickup and were on their way.

"I have a question," Rickie said.

"Shoot."

"I know that Poncho is actually Detective Adam Santiago. And you mentioned that Duck's name is Matt. How'd he get that nickname?"

"The cheerleaders used to tell Matt that he had a sexy stride. Poncho and I didn't want him to get too full of himself, so we told him we thought he walked like a duck. And the name stuck."

Rickie laughed. "I would have liked knowing you guys as teenagers."

At that, Clay laughed, too. "I don't know about that. You might not have liked us. We were pretty rowdy back then."

The pickup slowed, and Clay turned into the entrance to the Rocking C. They followed a long driveway to the ranch house, where a couple of elderly men sat in rockers on the big wraparound porch.

As they got out of the car and headed to the house, one of the old guys scrunched his brow and hollered out to Rickie. "I thought you went on a cruise, Lainie. What'd you do with Drew and the kids?"

"I'm not Lainie," she said. "I'm her twin sister, Erica."

"Well, I'll be damned." The balding old man wearing worn jeans and bedroom slippers got to his feet, reached for his cane and made his way toward her. After giving her a closer look, he chuckled. "You look exactly like her."

Before Rickie could respond, an older woman wearing an apron stepped out onto the porch. The moment she spotted Rickie, her lips parted. "Lainie… What happened? You're not supposed to…" She paused and scanned Rickie's length. Apparently, she noted the baby bump, because she laughed and said, "You must be Lainie's twin sister."

"That's right. I'm Erica Campbell."

"I'm so happy to finally meet you." The older woman, whose hair was a pretty shade of red, probably dyed, stepped off the porch and closed the gap between them. "Your sister told me all about you, and I'd been hoping and praying that she'd find you. I'm Joy Darnell, the ranch cook. My husband, Sam, is the foreman."

Rickie again introduced Clay as her friend, hoping he'd correct her, but he didn't.

"Lainie will be so sorry she missed you," Joy said.

"I knew she wouldn't be here. I was just so eager to connect with her that I wanted a chance to see where she used to live and to talk someone who knows her."

"Well, I'm glad you did. We love Lainie here, so it's a special treat to meet you. Would you like to stay for dinner? There's plenty for both of you."

"No, but thank you. We only stopped by for a minute. And to leave my phone number with you. Please let my sister know I was here, and if one of you will call me as soon as she gets home, I'll come back to the ranch to see her."

"Of course I will. It'll be my pleasure."

After saying their goodbyes, Rickie and Clay returned to his pickup and headed back to the clinic, where she'd left her car.

"Did it help you to visit the Rocking C?" Clay asked.

"Yes, it did. Thanks for taking me."

"No problem."

Rickie inhaled softly and slowly let it out, releasing the memories of past hurts and disappointment. Instead, she would focus on her many recent blessings. She seemed to be acquiring a long list of them.

"Now at Thanksgiving," she said, "when we sit around the table eating turkey and stuffing, I'll have one more thing to be thankful for."

Clay merely nodded and continued to drive.

Life was certainly coming together for her, and she had Clay to thank for that. Sandra, too. The woman had been more than kind. She'd welcomed Rickie into her home and her heart with open arms.

"I don't know if your mother told you," Rickie said, "but she invited me to stay at the Bar M after the babies come. That way she can babysit while I work. I told her I'd have to talk to you first."

"Seriously?" he asked.

The surprise in his tone was laced with irritation, which took her aback. "Is there a problem?"

"Not really. It's just that…" He sucked in a deep breath, then blew it out in an exaggerated huff. "My mom should have run that idea past me before talking to you."

Rickie flinched, and her heart crumpled. If Clay was upset that his mother issued the invitation to stay at the ranch, it was because he wouldn't have made the offer on his own. She probably should wait it out and let him explain, but that wasn't necessary.

"Don't worry," she said. "I won't take your mother up on the offer. That's why I told her that I'd talk it over with you first. But you've made it clear, once again, that you want to keep me at arm's distance."

Clay clicked his tongue and shot a glance across the seat at her. "That's not what I meant."

"Oh, no? I keep getting flashbacks of the other times you withdrew from me, starting when I visited you at Tripler. You practically ordered me from your hospital room."

"I was in pain. And I'd just received bad news."

She nodded. "I know. And at the time, I convinced myself that was the reason you were so rude and unfeeling. But now I know differently."

His brow furrowed and he cut another glance her way. "What are you talking about?"

She crossed her arms, resting them on her belly. "It's what you always do, Clay. Remember that day at the ranch, when I came to tell you about the babies? You were a jerk then, too."

"Oh, come on, Rickie. The news blindsided me."

"Yeah, I know. That's what you said when you apologized, and I bought your explanation then."

"It was the truth," he said.

"Only partially. But there's more to it than that. I gave you the benefit of the doubt before, but I'm not going to do that anymore. You don't deal very well with your emotions, and you pull away from anything or anyone who might force you to face what you're really feeling."

He gawked at her as if she'd blindsided him once again. But these days she needed someone who loved her, someone who would stick by her no matter what life threw their way. And a guy who skated around his emotions wasn't going to fit the bill.

Yet while she'd come to that easy conclusion and realized she needed to cut her losses, his harsh reaction, his rejection, still hurt something fierce, making it almost difficult to breathe.

"Like I told you before," she said, "I don't need you and I don't want anything from you. Whatever we had is over."

"Slow down, Rickie. You're getting all riled up. I never suggested ending things. At least, not completely."

There he went again, withdrawing. Building walls between them.

"No, Clay," she said. "It's better this way. I can't take the emotional roller coaster. But for the record, I plan to maintain a friendship with your mom. She'll be the grandmother to my kids, the only one they'll have. So I'm going to nurture a relationship that will benefit my children."

As Clay pulled into the clinic parking lot, he said, "You took my comment the wrong way."

"Did I?" She all but rolled her eyes and slowly shook her head. "I told you before. I can parent the twins on my own—and I can support them, too."

He swore under his breath. "You're letting your hormones get away from you."

"The hell I am. Don't minimize my feelings. At least I can face mine."

Clay parked next to her car and let his engine idle. "Let's talk about this when we get back to the ranch."

As emotion balled up in her throat, and tears filled her eyes, she turned away from him, unwilling to let him see how badly he'd hurt her. Without another word, she reached for her purse, got out and closed the passenger door. He didn't drive away. Instead, he waited for her to slide behind the wheel of her sedan and start the ignition. Only then did he put his truck in gear.

But instead of driving back to the Bar M, as he'd assumed she would, Rickie headed home, tears streaming down her face, her chest aching as if her heart had cracked right down the middle.

She meant what she'd said when she told Clay she could live without him in her life. And she would.

Only trouble was, she'd fallen in love with him. And it hurt something awful to realize her dreams of a loving relationship with her babies' father had been dashed.

Rickie continued to cry and grumble all the way to Jeffersville. When she got within a mile of city limits, a flatbed truck loaded down with hay pulled out in front of her and made a turn to the right. The bales hadn't been tied down properly, so they shifted. Several tumbled onto the street.

Rickie swerved to avoid them, but the car spun out of control, swirling her around like a carnival ride until she slammed into a light pole.

Dazed, she tried to think, to react. But her head hurt. When she reached up and fingered her brow, she felt the sticky flow of blood. She blinked a couple of times, trying to clear her thoughts.

A sharp cramp struck low in her belly, tightening. She adjusted the seat belt, hoping that would help it ease up.

Someone—his face was a blur—opened the driver's door. "Lady, are you okay?"

She nodded, but apparently he didn't believe her. He whipped out his cell phone and called 911.

Minutes later, another pain sliced low in her belly. A contraction? Something was terribly wrong.

Fear gripped her like never before. God help her. If she was going to lose the babies, she needed a hand to hold. Clay probably wouldn't approve, but she didn't give a rip about that. She'd grown close to his mother, who'd become a friend—and the only one she had, it seemed. So she fumbled in her purse and pulled out her cell phone, then called Sandra.

By the time she answered, Rickie heard sirens in the distance. "I've been in a car accident. I'm going to be taken to the hospital in Jeffersville. Will you please come?"

"Oh my God. Are you okay?"

"I...don't know. I think so."

"I'll be right there, sweetie. Does Clay know? If not, I'll call him on his cell."

"Please don't. We had a big fight, and I'd rather he didn't know anything about this."

Sandra paused. "Don't worry. You have enough to worry about, so I won't. I'm just grabbing my keys and leaving now."

"Thank you, Sandra. I don't know what I'd do without you."

"Everything will be fine. I'm sure of it."

Maybe so, but right now, with fear of losing the babies gripping her, she had every reason to doubt that things would ever be okay again.

Chapter Twelve

After ordering a large cup of black coffee and a choc-olate éclair at Poncho's favorite doughnut shop, Clay took a seat across the white Formica table from his old high school friend. They sat in silence for a moment or two until Poncho finally asked, "So what was it you wanted to talk about?"

Clay blew out a weary sigh. "Rickie and I got into an argument earlier today. I tried to apologize—or explain—but she didn't want to hear it."

Poncho took a sip of coffee. "So you're looking for a voice of reason?"

"Pretty much." Clay needed to vent to someone he trusted.

"So what upset her?"

"To begin with, my mom and Rickie have become best friends, which doesn't sit well with me."

Poncho eyed Clay the way a highway patrolman assessed the driver of a speeding car. "Why would that bother you? I'd think it would make your life a lot easier."

"Maybe it will." Clay reached for his heat-resistant paper cup, yet he didn't take a drink. "But for some crazy reason, it feels like they're plotting something behind my back."

Poncho leaned forward. "Like what?"

"I don't know. Nothing yet. But it won't take long. They'll team up against me one of these days." Clay raked his hand through his hair. "Now *me*? I can handle whatever comes my way. But what about the twins? Those two women are going to try and put the kibosh on everything those kids want to do."

Poncho sat back, a wry grin tickling his lips. "You managed to rebel and do your own thing."

"Yeah, but it was always an uphill battle." Clay took a bite of his éclair, but the chocolaty treat did little to soften or sweeten his mood. "When Rickie told me that my mother had invited her to live at the ranch after the babies were born, that really sent me over the edge."

"I can see where you'd be upset about her moving in when you're not sure how you feel about her." Poncho took another sip of coffee. When Clay didn't respond, he asked, "How *do* you feel about her?"

"I care about her. A lot. She's sweet and funny. And the sex is out of this world."

"It sounds to me like you're falling for her."

Clay pondered that possibility for a beat. "Maybe so, but I don't want to rush things. And my mom has always tried to force my hand."

"Forgive me for not seeing your mom as the villain in all of this. She's a great lady. And you're lucky to have someone who loves you like that, even if she still tries too hard to keep you on the straight and narrow."

Guilt thumped Clay like a wallop to the chest. "I'm sorry. I shouldn't complain, especially to you."

"I might've had a crappy upbringing," Poncho said, "but I've seen a lot of kids who've had it worse. And you, my friend, had it *good*. If you doubt that, I'll take you on a tour to Kidville, the children's home, and introduce you to some of the little boys I mentor."

Poncho was right. Clay really didn't have anything to complain about. But the flight mishap had sent him into a tailspin, and he'd been trying to recover control of his life ever since. He took a sip of coffee. It was supposed to be a fresh brew, but it had a bitter taste.

As things began to fall into perspective, Clay felt even worse than when he'd walked into the Donut Hole. Instead of his frustration with Rickie, he now had to deal with his guilt.

"Did you tell her you wanted to take things slow?" Poncho asked.

"Sort of." Actually, he'd meant to. "This whole thing has me unbalanced, and I have to admit that I didn't handle it very well."

Poncho laughed. "I hear that love can really throw a man off stride."

Clay grunted. Damn. Not only had he acted like a Neanderthal, he sounded like one, too.

But the more he thought about it, the more he realized Poncho might be right.

"I'm not sure if it's love, but I have some pretty strong feelings for her. I guess I'd better apologize. She must think I'm an ass."

"Probably, but if you tell her how you're really feeling, I think she'll forgive you."

"That's the problem. I was going to try to explain, but she didn't let me. Instead, she flipped out."

"Let me guess," Poncho said. "You went for the just-one-of-the-guys approach. Not a good idea, man. Women are wired differently. They're more in touch with their feelings, and it can really ruffle them when a guy isn't being honest with his emotions or with whatever he has on his mind. And you, my friend, are pretty tight-lipped when it comes to stuff like that."

"Tell me about it." Clay pushed aside the éclair, deciding it had looked a lot more appetizing in the glass display case than it actually tasted. "Believe it or not, I probably would have come to that conclusion on the way to the ranch. And then I could have told her, if she'd followed me there, like I thought she'd do. But she turned right and headed for the interstate. I'm pretty sure she drove back to Jeffersville."

Poncho crossed his arms. "Sounds to me like you ran her off."

"I didn't mean to."

"She'll come around."

Clay wasn't too sure about that. "She made it pretty clear that she didn't need me—now or in the future. And maybe that's true. Hell, she's just reconnected with her sister—at least, she's located her, and soon she'll get to see her for the first time in years. So she won't be alone anymore. She has a real family to rely on now."

"You know what I think?"

Clay had called Poncho so he could blow off some steam. And he'd expected his friend to tell him he was right. Although he was getting the feeling that wasn't what he was going to hear. "Go ahead and tell me."

"You've been running scared of family-type commitments for as long as I've known you. And you're afraid that a solid sense of home and hearth is going to change things. And it will. But in your case, I think it's a good thing."

Clay was going to have to chew on that for a while. He glanced across the table at his friend, who was staring at him like he was a suspect in an interrogation room.

"What do *you* think?" Poncho asked.

"You've got a point." More than one, actually. Clay found himself thinking about Rickie all the time, and whenever he did, a warm feeling filled his chest. He liked being with her. And he wanted to make life easier for her.

As reality dawned, he had to face the truth. And as tough as it might be, he'd have to lay his cards on the table, starting with Poncho.

"Okay," Clay said. "I'll admit it. My feelings for Rickie are too strong for my comfort level. And ignoring them has made it worse."

"So what are you going to do about that?"

"I'm going to let her cool off for a bit. Then I'll drive to her house and apologize."

"Sounds like a wise decision. And I recommend taking some flowers. You owe her, dude."

Clay didn't take time to finish his coffee. Instead, he pushed back his chair and got to his feet. "I'm going home. Thanks for talking me off the ledge."

"Hey. That's what friends are for."

Ten minutes later, Clay arrived at the ranch. He didn't see Rickie's car, indicating he'd been right—she'd gone home to Jeffersville. But that didn't mean he couldn't apologize to his mom first. Over the years, he'd built walls to keep her at a distance, and not always in subtle ways.

He'd start by telling her that he loved her, that he appreciated her unabashed acceptance of Rickie. And that he was going to try to be more understanding of her motherly ways in the future.

But the moment he walked into the kitchen and spotted Granddad warming a can of chili beans on the stove, he realized his mother wasn't home. And that wasn't like her.

"Where's Mom?" he asked.

"She left a note for you on the table."

Clay snatched it and read his mother's handwriting. "Oh, God." His heart sank to the pit of his gut, and his thoughts spun out of control.

He looked at his grandfather, as if the older man could fix this situation, but he couldn't. "Rickie's been in a car accident. She's at the hospital."

He hadn't needed to tell his grandfather. The note had been open and in plain sight. Or else he'd been here when Mom left.

"Why didn't someone call me?" Clay asked.

"Rickie asked your mom not to, and I figured I'd better respect that."

"Dammit. I've gotta go."

"That'd be a good idea, son. She's at Jeffersville Memorial. Your mother should be with her by now."

For once, Clay was grateful for his mother's constant presence—he'd never want Rickie to be alone at a time like this. "Thanks, Granddad. I'm heading there right now."

Clay hurried out of the house, jumped into his pickup and drove as fast as he could without risking a ticket or an accident of his own.

This was all his fault. If he'd kept his mouth shut or chosen his words more carefully, Rickie would have gone home with him as planned. He hoped her injuries weren't serious, that she and the babies had survived the crash. He couldn't stand the thought of losing them—any of them.

Clay pushed down on the gas pedal, determined to get to his new little family as fast as he could.

Paramedics wasted no time in rushing Rickie to the hospital, where the ER doctor diagnosed a concussion then sutured her head wound. Her obstetrician arrived minutes later and examined her, too. Dr. Gomez also checked the babies' heart rates, which were strong and healthy. Then she ordered medication to stop labor, although the contractions had already eased a bit.

After their consultation, both medical professionals decided Rickie should stay overnight for observation.

Rickie wasn't about to argue that decision. She was just glad to know the twins were okay. It had been scary for a while. But from the moment of impact and all during the ambulance ride to the hospital, she'd held her panic at bay.

Yet the minute Clay's mother entered the room, with her brow furrowed and maternal concern splashed on her face, tears filled Rickie's eyes and a lump of emotion balled up in her throat.

"I got here as fast as I could," Sandra said. "Honey, are you okay?"

You. The woman's first thought had been about her, not just the twins. That meant that whatever maternal affection Rickie had sensed from Sandra was real. And not only an attempt to have a relationship with her grandbabies.

"Yes," Rickie said. "I'm all right. And so are the twins."

"Thank God. I prayed all the way here." Sandra, who was now standing beside the hospital bed, took Rickie's hand and gave it a gentle squeeze.

That loving gesture touched Rickie's heart, and in spite of her best efforts to hold herself together, the tears overflowed and spilled down her cheeks. Before she could thank Sandra for coming, for responding so quickly to her distressed phone call, Clay entered the room. He appeared worried and deeply concerned, but she wouldn't let that weaken her resolve.

"What happened?" he asked. "Are you all right, Rickie?"

She swiped at her wet cheeks and lifted her chin. "Yes. I'm fine."

"I know you're angry with me," he said. "And you have every right to be. I was an ass."

"Yes, you were. Apology accepted. So feel free to go on about your day."

The corner of his eye twitched, indicating her curt brush-off had hurt.

"All right," he said. "I'll go. But not until you let me explain."

Rickie glanced first at Sandra, who continued to hold her hand, watching the two of them while clearly biting her tongue. Then she returned her gaze to Clay. "I'm listening, but my response will be the same."

He blew out a ragged sigh. "I did some soul searching and realized a few things. Over the years, I built a wall around my emotions. I considered them a sign of weakness. So the idea of having a wife and kids has always scared the heck out of me. It would make me too vulnerable."

Rickie had figured as much. It was nice that he could admit it, although that didn't make her feel any better about pinning her heart on him. But she let him continue to get things off his chest.

"When you came to town, pregnant with not just one baby, but two, I scrambled to make sense of how I felt—about you, about us, about becoming a family. It's not a good excuse, but it's the only one I have. And the truth is, I love you, Rickie."

She wanted to believe him, but she'd been abandoned before. And Clay had disappointed her several times already. If she didn't have the babies to consider, she might have given him a pass. But she couldn't take a gamble like that. Not when he might harden his heart and hurt the kids someday.

He made his way into the room, although he maintained a respectful distance. "When I heard about the accident, reality slammed into me. I was afraid I'd lose you—and the babies. At that point, I finally felt some of what my mom went through when my dad died. She'd been devastated, and I can see why she'd be afraid to lose me, too. As a kid, I thought she was smothering me. But she only wanted to protect me. I get that now."

Sandra's eyes welled with tears, and she nodded, confirming the conclusion he'd come to.

"I might have gone a little overboard at times," she admitted, "but son, I love you more than life itself."

"I realize that now, Mom. And I'm sorry. I'm going to be a lot more understanding of your feelings from here on out."

Apparently, he thought Rickie should be more understanding, too. But even though she wanted to believe that he'd had some kind of emotional epiphany, she was afraid to. He'd flip-flopped on her one time too many.

Sandra gave her son a warm hug, letting him and Rickie know that she forgave him, that she loved him and always would.

Rickie wasn't going to be as easy to appease as his mother was.

As Clay eased closer to the hospital bed, his mom took a step back, allowing him to take her place at Rickie's side. "If you'll give me another chance, I'll step up and be the man you want me to be."

But could he be the man she *needed* him to be? It all

sounded good. He was saying the right words, but she wasn't convinced that he'd follow through. On top of that, her head ached. This wasn't the time to make any emotional decisions.

Rickie glanced at Sandra, who'd taken so many steps back that she'd almost left the room. Then she looked at Clay. "I'll need to think about it."

"That's all I'm asking for, Rickie. Just think about it."

She already had, and she'd made a tentative decision. Actually, it was pretty solid, but the pain meds might be skewing her thoughts. Either way, she thanked Clay for coming, then said, "It's probably best if you go now."

"Okay. I will, but I'll be back. I also want you to keep in mind the babies are going to need a father."

Maybe so. But it would be better for them to never know him than to bond with a guy who might get tired of playing the dad role and leave.

Clay hadn't wanted to leave Rickie's room, but he hadn't wanted to upset her, either. So he'd agreed to give her the time she needed and headed down the hospital corridor, determined to prove to her that he'd been telling the truth. And if that meant he'd have to drive all the way to Jeffersville each day, bearing a bouquet of roses and pouring out his heart, he'd do it.

It was weird, though. He'd been dodging his feelings for years, but facing them actually made him feel better. More focused, more secure.

Rather than stray too far from Rickie's bedside, he went to the hospital cafeteria and bought a large coffee. Then he took it to the main lobby, where he took a seat with several other people who were either reading magazines or watching TV while they waited for word on a loved one's condition.

He'd no more than taken a couple of drinks when his cell phone rang. He glanced at the screen and saw that it was his mom calling.

"I just stepped into the hall so I could call you. I've been talking to Rickie, and it might be a good idea if you came back to the hospital. I think she's having a change of heart."

He'd hoped she would. That's why he hadn't gone far. "What makes you think that?"

"We had a little chat about your father and how, in spite of his imperfections, I loved him. I told her that I'd give anything if he could be here now, if he could meet her. And that he would have been thrilled to know he was going to be a grandfather."

"What did she say to that?"

"That she loved you. And that she thought you'd be a good father."

"Thanks for the heads-up. I'll be there in five minutes."

"In that case, I'll go to the cafeteria so I can give you two some time to talk in private."

Had his mother always been that intuitive, that understanding? That supportive?

By the time Clay returned to Rickie's room, she was alone. Her face was angled toward the window, as if she was gazing outside. When she heard footsteps, she turned to face the doorway, where he stood. She didn't exactly break into a grin when she spotted him, but she didn't send him away, either.

"Is it okay if I come in?" he asked.

She nodded.

He took a slow approach. "I realize things are a little crazy right now."

"Yeah, they are." She offered him a weak, tentative grin. "Part of it might be the pain medication they gave me."

"And another part is because I was a jerk."

"Yeah, that, too." This time a full-on smile crossed her face, and he realized his mother had been right. Rickie had been thinking—and reconsidering.

"I'm really sorry," he told her. "If you give me a second chance, I promise to do better in the future."

"You know," she said, "I spent years believing my sister was dead. Her loss crushed me. The more I thought about it, the more I realized I was about to suffer another loss—the man I love."

"If I'm that man," Clay said, "I'm not going anywhere. And just to set the record straight, I'm glad my mother invited you to stay on the ranch with us. I'd like you and our kids to be close."

"Are you sure?"

He nodded. "Yes, but there's something else I want to tell you, something I've kept to myself, but you should probably know. Part of my moodiness and negativity had to do with the fact that I never wanted to be a rancher in the first place. But that's the way things panned out. I've accepted it, and I'm going to make the best of it."

"But that ranch has been in your family for years. What is it you'd rather do?"

He took a deep, fortifying breath, then let it and the raw truth slip out. "I'd like to do what I was trained to do, what I love."

She nodded knowingly. "And after that flight mishap and your injury, the Army is out."

"Yes, and so is being a pilot for a Life Flight helicopter, a local job that's opening up. It would've been a cool, home-based option."

"Why can't you take it?" she asked.

"The damage to my optic nerve. Remember?"

Her brow furrowed, tightening the stitches on her head wound. She winced, then asked, "When was your last eye exam?"

"When I was at Tripler."

"No kidding? Haven't you had a follow-up?"

"I…uh… No."

She scrunched her brow and winced again. "Why not?"

"I guess I was afraid to hear another repeat of that crappy diagnosis."

"For a guy who's always been Army strong, you're pretty weak when it comes to facing your emotional side."

"You're right. And I'm facing it now. I love you, Rickie. I want to spend the rest of my life with you, raising our children." He paused, waiting a beat before posing the question he'd been thinking about for the past hour or two. "Will you marry me?"

She seemed to ponder that for the longest time, and when he feared she might blow him off, she smiled and said, "Yes, I'll marry you. I love you, too. But I think we'd both be better off if we took our relationship one day at a time."

That's all he'd hoped for, all he'd wanted to hear. He bent over her bed and gave her a kiss. It might've been gentle and a bit hesitant, but it was filled with promise— and commitment.

When he straightened, she said, "So tell me. When are you going to have your vision checked again?"

He hadn't planned on doing that, but with Rickie suggesting it, he figured he ought to face his limitations, too. "I guess that depends on when Dr. Davidson will refer me to an ophthalmologist or neurologist."

Rickie laughed. "The receptionist has quite a bit of pull, so I'm sure she'll have a name and phone number for you first thing tomorrow morning."

Clay kissed this amazing woman again. How had he ever gotten by without her in his life, his arms or his bed?

"I have a question," she said. "I know it was my idea, but maybe we shouldn't take things too slowly. It might be a good idea to get married before the babies come."

"I was hoping you'd come to feel that way, too. I'd marry you tomorrow, but we'll probably need a license."

She laughed once more, then reached for him, drawing his lips to hers. He kissed her again, and his heart as well as his dreams took flight.

For the first time since his accident, he looked forward to the future, one that promised to be happy and bright.

Epilogue

A week after Rickie came home from the hospital, Lainie and her husband, rodeo promoter Drew Madison, and their children arrived home after their Disney cruise. When Lainie heard that her lost twin was looking for her and had left her phone number, she immediately placed the call.

Lainie shrieked with joy and excitement. "You have no idea how much I've missed you."

"Oh, yes I do!" Rickie's voice held the same thrill. "I was told that you died during your surgery. I was devastated to hear that, and I've been grieving for years. Imagine my surprise when I learned you were alive."

There were happy tears shed, and some sad ones, as they tried to play catch up after so many years apart.

Sandra, who'd been standing nearby when the heartwarming phone call took place, listened with a smile and glistening eyes. When she heard the sisters' planning to meet the next day and introduce their new families, she suggested they have a picnic.

"That way," Sandra had said, "we can have a meet and greet during your reunion."

Both sisters liked the idea, especially since the new Brighton Valley Park had an amazing playground the children would enjoy.

And now here they were. Rickie brought her new family, which included Clay, his mother and grandfather. Soon Lainie, Drew and their three sons would be drawn into the fold.

Clay, who'd been helping his mother carry the food and picnic supplies from the car, joined Rickie where she stood in the shade of a magnolia tree, watching the street and waiting for her sister to arrive. He slipped an arm around her waist and gave her an affectionate squeeze. "How are you doing? It's a little chilly. Do you want me to get your sweater?"

"No, I'm fine. In fact, I've never been better." She leaned into him, placed her head against his shoulder and relished his familiar scent.

"My mom is putting out a big spread," he said.

"I know." Rickie couldn't believe the woman's energy. Early this morning, she'd made potato salad, baked beans and a huge fruit bowl, insisting she didn't want help. At least she'd let Rickie bring dessert—cupcakes she and Clay purchased at a local bakery.

Even Roger, who'd asked Rickie to call him Granddad from now on, would be doing his part, cooking hamburgers and hot dogs on a small stationary grill.

"I'd better see if my grandfather needs help," Clay said.

"Have you talked to him yet?" Rickie asked.

"Yes, I did. Right before we left the ranch." Clay had passed the eye exam, although just barely. And he'd accepted the job as a Life Flight pilot.

"How'd he take it?"

"A lot better than I thought he would. He told me that he really hadn't wanted to retire in the first place, but my mom had encouraged it. 'You know how she is,' he said. I would have agreed and rolled my eyes, but for the first time, I found myself saying, 'She means well.'"

"Maybe, on your days off, you can help out on the ranch."

"Yes, I plan to. That is, unless I'm busy being a father." Clay placed his hand on her baby bump. "How are the kids doing?"

"They're a little restless today," she said. "I think they're eager to get out and meet their new cousins."

"Speaking of introductions, have we decided on their names for sure? Are we going to stick with Jonathon and Katherine?"

"Yes, but those are pretty long names for tiny babies. What if we call them John and Katie?"

"That works for me." Clay nodded toward Granddad. "I'd better see if he needs help setting up that grill." Then he brushed a kiss on her brow before walking away.

At the sound of an approaching vehicle, Rickie turned and spotted an SUV entering the parking lot. It looked like a dad, mom and three little boys. That must be Lainie, she thought.

When a brunette climbed out of the front passenger seat, she noted the resemblance and realized she was right.

As Lainie crossed the grass, leaving her husband to help the younger boys get out of their car seats, Rickie hurried to meet her.

"Can you believe it?" Lainie said, her smile beaming. "I never thought this day would come."

Rickie laughed. "Neither did I. You have no idea how much I've missed you. How many times I've thought about you over the years. I'm so glad we finally found each other."

Lainie slipped her arms around Rickie and gave her a hug, one they both were reluctant to end. So they continued to hold each other, their heads touching, their hair the same shade, the length similar. They'd always looked alike, but when Rickie had been the healthier twin, people didn't have any trouble telling them apart. However, that wasn't the case any longer. That is, unless someone looked at their stomachs.

Everyone seemed to be giving them space and time to reunite, but before long, three adorable, dark-haired boys joined them.

"Hey, Mama!" the oldest one said. "There's two of you!"

"You're right," Lainie told her son. "This is my sister—and your aunt."

"I'm so happy to meet you guys," Rickie said, as she stooped to shake each small hand. There'd be plenty of time for hugs and kisses—once they got to know her better. And that wouldn't take long. She planned to be the best aunt ever.

Andre, the oldest had a walking cast on his leg, thanks to a recent orthopedic surgery to correct a bone that hadn't healed properly. But that didn't seem to keep the eight-year-old sidelined.

From what Lainie had said last night, their early years had been rough, but they had a new home and loving parents now. Andre and his younger brothers, Mario and Abel, were as cute as they could be. And they were clearly happy and thriving.

"Can we go play now?" Mario asked.

Lainie caressed her son's head. "Yes, of course."

As the boys dashed off, Rickie glanced across the grass and watched Sandra cover a table with a red-checkered cloth. "You know, I'd better insist upon helping my future mother-in-law."

"And I'd better get the kids' jackets. I don't want them to catch cold. When one gets the sniffles, they all do."

As Lainie strode toward the car, Rickie approached the woman who claimed she was the daughter she'd always wanted. "You're spoiling me, Sandra. Please let me do something to help."

Sandra brightened. "It's nearly done. I love cooking for my family, but I'm really going to enjoy it now that our family has grown. I can't wait for Thanksgiving and Christmas. They're going to be extra-special days from now on."

Rickie agreed. The upcoming holidays promised to be big, happy affairs. She stole a glance at Clay, who'd wandered over to the playground and was pushing little

Mario in the swing. Not only was that gorgeous man an amazing lover, but he promised to be a wonderful husband, father and uncle.

She placed her hand on her growing womb and smiled. For the very first time, she could imagine living happily ever after.

* * * * *

Don't miss the next installment of
ROCKING CHAIR RODEO
by USA TODAY *bestselling author Judy Duarte*
On sale January 2019
Wherever Harlequin books and ebooks are sold!

And catch up with the cowboys—and cowgirls!—on
the Rocking Chair Ranch

Look for

ROPING IN THE COWGIRL
THE BRONC RIDER'S BABY
and
A COWBOY FAMILY CHRISTMAS
Available now!

Turn the page for a sneak peek at the latest entry in
New York Times *bestselling author*
RaeAnne Thayne's HAVEN POINT *series,*
THE COTTAGES ON SILVER BEACH, the story of a
disgraced FBI agent, his best friend's sister and the
loss that affected the trajectory of both their lives,
available July 2018 wherever HQN books
and ebooks are sold!

CHAPTER ONE

SOMEONE WAS TRYING to bust into the cottages next door.

Only minutes earlier, Megan Hamilton had been minding her own business, sitting on her front porch, gazing out at the stars and enjoying the peculiar quiet sweetness of a late-May evening on Lake Haven. She had earned this moment of peace after working all day at the inn's front desk then spending the last four hours at her computer, editing photographs from Joe and Lucy White's 50th anniversary party the weekend before.

Her neck was sore, her shoulders tight, and she simply wanted to savor the purity of the evening with her dog at her feet. Her moment of Zen had lasted only sixty seconds before her little ancient pug Cyrus sat up, gazed out into the darkness and gave one small harrumphing noise before settling back down again to watch as a vehicle pulled up to the cottage next door.

Cyrus had become used to the comings and goings of their guests in the two years since he and Megan moved into the cottage after the inn's renovations were finished. She would venture to say her pudgy little dog seemed to actually enjoy the parade of strangers who invariably stopped to greet him.

The man next door wasn't aware of her presence,

though, or that of her little pug. He was too busy trying to work the finicky lock—not an easy feat as the task typically took two hands and one of his appeared to be attached to an arm tucked into a sling.

She should probably go help him. He was obviously struggling one-handed, unable to turn the key and twist the knob at the same time.

Beyond common courtesy, there was another compelling reason she should probably get off her porch swing and assist him. He was a guest of the inn, which meant he was yet one more responsibility on her shoulders. She knew the foibles of that door handle well, since she owned the door, the porch, the house and the land that it sat on, here at Silver Beach on Lake Haven, part of the extensive grounds of the Inn at Haven Point.

She didn't want to help him. She wanted to stay right here hidden in shadows, trying to pretend he wasn't there. Maybe this was all a bad dream and she wouldn't be stuck with him for the next three weeks.

Megan closed her eyes, wishing she could open them again and find the whole thing was a figment of her imagination.

Unfortunately, it was all entirely too real. Elliot Bailey. Living next door.

She didn't want him here. Stupid online bookings. If he had called in person about renting the cottage next to hers—one of five small, charming two-bedroom vacation rentals along the lakeshore—she might have been able to concoct some excuse.

With her imagination, surely she could have come up with something good. All the cottages were being painted. A plumbing issue meant none of them had water. The entire place had to be fumigated for tarantulas.

If she had spoken with him in person, she may have been able to concoct *some* excuse that would keep Elliot Bailey away. But he had used the inn's online reservation system and paid in full before she even realized who was moving in next door. Now she was stuck with him for three entire weeks.

She would have to make the best of it.

As he tried the door again, guilt poked at her. Even if she didn't want him here, she couldn't sit here when one of her guests needed help. It was rude, selfish and irresponsible. "Stay," she murmured to Cyrus, then stood up and made her way down the porch steps of Primrose Cottage and back up those of Cedarwood.

"May I help?"

At her words, Elliot whirled around, the fingers of his right hand flexing inside his sling as if reaching for a weapon. She had to hope he didn't have one. Maybe she should have thought of that before sneaking up on him.

Elliot was a decorated FBI agent and always exuded an air of cold danger, as if ready to strike at any moment. It was as much a part of him as his blue eyes.

His brother had shared the same eyes, but the similarities between them ended there. Wyatt's blue eyes had been warm, alive, brimming with personality. Elliot's were serious and solemn and always seemed to look at her as if she were some kind of alien life-form that had landed in his world.

Her heart gave a familiar pinch at the thought of

Wyatt and the fledgling dreams that had been taken away from her on a snowy road.

"Megan," he said, his voice as stiff and formal as if he were greeting J. Edgar Hoover himself. "I didn't see you."

"It's a dark evening and I'm easy to miss. I didn't mean to startle you."

In the yellow glow of the porch light, his features appeared lean and alert, like a hungry mountain lion. She could feel her muscles tense in response, a helpless doe caught unawares in an alpine meadow.

She adored the rest of the Bailey family. All of them, even linebacker-big Marshall. Why was Elliot the only one who made her so blasted nervous?

"May I help you?" she asked again. "This lock can be sticky. Usually it takes two hands, one to twist the key and the other to pull the door toward you."

"That could be an issue for the next three weeks." His voice seemed flat and she had the vague, somewhat disconcerting impression that he was tired. Elliot always seemed so invincible but now lines bracketed his mouth and his hair was uncharacteristically rumpled. It seemed so odd to see him as anything other than perfectly controlled.

Of course he was tired. The man had just driven in from Denver. Anybody would be exhausted after an eight-hour drive—especially when he was healing from an obvious injury and probably in pain.

What happened to his arm? She wanted to ask, but couldn't quite find the courage. It wasn't her business anyway. Elliot was a guest of her inn and deserved all the hospitality she offered to any guest—including whatever privacy he needed and help accessing the cottage he had paid in advance to rent.

"There is a trick," she told him. "If you pull the door slightly toward you first, then turn the key, you should be able to manage with one hand. If you have trouble again, you can find me or one of the staff to help you. I live next door."

The sound he made might have been a laugh or a scoff. She couldn't tell.

"Of course you do."

She frowned. What did that mean? With all the renovations to the inn after a devastating fire, she couldn't afford to pay for an overnight manager. It had seemed easier to move into one of the cottages so she could be close enough to step in if the front desk clerks had a problem in the middle of the night.

That's the only reason she was here. Elliot didn't need to respond to that information as if she was some loser who hadn't been able to fly far from the nest.

"We need someone on-site full-time to handle emergencies," she said stiffly. "Such as guests who can't open their doors by themselves."

"I am certainly not about to bother you or your staff every time I need to go in and out of my own rental unit. I'll figure something out."

His voice sounded tight, annoyed, and she tried to attribute it to travel weariness instead of that subtle disapproval she always seemed to feel emanating from him.

"I can help you this time at least." She inserted his key, exerted only a slight amount of pull on the door and heard the lock disengage. She pushed the door open and flipped on a light inside the cheery little two-bedroom cottage, with its small combined living-dining room and kitchen table set in front of the big windows over-looking the lake.

"Thank you for your help," he said, sounding a little less censorious.

"Anytime." She smiled her well-practiced, smooth, innkeeper smile. After a decade of running the twenty-room Inn at Haven Point on her own, she had become quite adept at exuding hospitality she was far from feel-ing.

"May I help you with your bags?"

He gave her a long, steady look that conveyed clearly what he thought of that offer. "I'm good. Thanks."

She shrugged. Stubborn man. Let him struggle. "Good night, then. If you need anything, you know where to find me."

"Yes. I do. Next door, apparently."

"That's right. Good night," she said again, then re-turned to her front porch, where she and Cyrus settled in to watch him pull a few things out of his vehicle and carry them inside.

She could have saved him a few trips up and down those steps, but clearly he wanted to cling to his own stubbornness instead. As usual, it was obvious he wanted nothing to do with her. Elliot tended to treat her as if she were a riddle he had no desire to solve.

Over the years, she had developed pretty good strat-egies for avoiding him at social gatherings, though it was a struggle. She had once been almost engaged to his younger brother. That alone would tend to link her to the Bailey family, but it wasn't the only tie between them. She counted his sisters, Wynona Bailey Emmett and Katrina Bailey Callahan, among her closest friends.

In fact, because of her connection to his sisters, she knew he was in town at least partly to attend a big after-the-fact reception to celebrate Katrina's wedding to Bowie Callahan, which had been a small destination event in Colombia several months earlier.

Megan had known Elliot for years. Though only five or six years older, somehow he had always seemed ancient to her, even when she was a girl—as if he belonged to some earlier generation. He was so serious all the time, like some sort of stuffy uncle who couldn't be bothered with youthful shenanigans.

Hey, you kids. Get off my lawn.

He'd probably never actually said those words, but she could clearly imagine them coming out of that incongruously sexy mouth.

He did love his family. She couldn't argue that. He watched out for his sisters and was close to his brother Marshall, the sheriff of Lake Haven County. He cherished his mother and made the long trip from Denver to Haven Point for every important Bailey event, several times a year.

Which also begged the question, why had he chosen to rent a cottage on the inn property instead of staying with one of his family members?

His mother and stepfather lived not far away and so did Marshall, Wynona and Katrina with their respective spouses. While Marshall's house was filled to the brim with kids, Cade and Wyn had plenty of room and Bowie and Katrina had a vast house on Serenity Harbor that would fit the entire Haven Point High School football team, with room left over for the coaching staff and a few cheerleaders.

Instead, Elliot had chosen to book this small, solitary rental unit at the inn for three entire weeks.

Did his reasons have anything to do with that sling? How had he been hurt? Did it have anything to do with his work for the FBI?

None of her business, Megan reminded herself. He was a guest at her inn, which meant she had an obligation to respect his privacy.

He came back to the vehicle for one more bag, something that looked the size of a laptop, which gave her something else to consider. He had booked the cottage for three weeks. Maybe he had taken a leave of absence or something to work on another book.

She pulled Cyrus into her lap and rubbed behind his ears as she considered the cottage next door and the enigmatic man currently inhabiting it. Whoever would have guessed that the stiff, humorless, focused FBI agent could pen gripping true crime books in his spare time? She would never admit it to Elliot, but she found it utterly fascinating how his writing managed to convey pathos and drama and even some lighter moments.

True crime was definitely not her groove at all but she had read his last bestseller in five hours, without so much as stopping to take a bathroom break—and had slept with her closet light on for weeks.

That still didn't mean she wanted him living next door. At this point, she couldn't do anything to change that. The only thing she could do was treat him with the same courtesy and respect she would any other guest at the inn.

No matter how difficult that might prove.

WHAT THE HELL was he doing here?

Elliot dragged his duffel to the larger of the cottage's two bedrooms, where a folding wood-framed luggage stand had been set out, ready for guests.

The cottage was tastefully decorated in what he termed Western chic—bold mission furniture, wood plank ceiling, colorful rugs on the floor. A river rock fireplace dominated the living room, probably perfect for those chilly evenings along the lakeshore.

Cedarwood Cottage seemed comfortable and welcoming, a good place for him to huddle over his laptop and pound out the last few chapters of the book that was overdue to his editor.

Even so, he could already tell this was a mistake.

Why the hell hadn't he just told his mother and Katrina he couldn't make it to the reception? He'd flown to Cartagena for the wedding three months earlier, after all. Surely that showed enough personal commitment to his baby sister's nuptials.

They would have protested but would have understood—and in the end it wouldn't have much mattered whether he made it home for the event or not. The reception wasn't about him, it was about Bowie and Katrina and the life they were building with Bowie's younger brother Milo and Kat's adopted daughter, Gabriella.

For his part, Elliot was quite sure he would have been better off if he had stayed holed up in his condo in Denver to finish the book, no matter how awkward things had become for him there. If he closed the blinds, ignored the doorbell and just hunkered down, he could have typed one-handed or even dictated the changes he needed to make. The whole thing would have been done in a week.

The manuscript wasn't the problem.

Elliot frowned, his head pounding in rhythm to each throbbing ache of his shoulder.

He was the problem—and he couldn't escape the mess he had created, no matter how far away from Denver he drove.

He struggled to unzip the duffel one-handed, then finally gave up and stuck his right arm out of the sling to help. His shoulder ached even more in response, not happy with being subjected to eight hours of driving only days postsurgery.

How was he going to explain the shoulder injury to his mother? He couldn't tell her he was recovering from a gunshot wound. Charlene had lost a son and husband in the line of duty and had seen both a daughter and her other son injured on the job.

And he certainly couldn't tell Marshall or Cade about all the trouble he was in. He was the model FBI agent, with the unblemished record.

Until now.

Unpacking took him all of five minutes, moving the

packing cubes into drawers, setting his toiletries in the bathroom, hanging the few dress shirts he had brought along. When he was done, he wandered back into the combined living room/kitchen.

The front wall was made almost entirely of windows, perfect for looking out and enjoying the spectacular view of Lake Haven during one of its most beautiful seasons, late spring, before the tourist horde descended.

On impulse, Elliot walked out onto the wide front porch. The night was chilly but the mingled scents of pine and cedar and lake intoxicated him. He drew fresh mountain air deep into his lungs.

This.

If he needed to look for a reason why he had been compelled to come home during his suspension and the investigation into his actions, he only had to think about what this view would look like in the morning, with the sun creeping over the mountains.

Lake Haven called to him like nowhere else on Earth—not just the stunning blue waters or the mountains that jutted out of them in jagged peaks but the calm, rhythmic lapping of the water against the shore, the ever-changing sky, the cry of wood ducks pedaling in for a landing.

He had spent his entire professional life digging into the worst aspects of the human condition, investigating cruelty and injustice and people with no moral conscience whatsoever. No matter what sort of muck he waded through, he had figured out early in his career at the FBI that he could keep that ugliness from touching the core of him with thoughts of Haven Point and the people he loved who called this place home.

He didn't visit as often as he would like. Between his job at the Denver field office and the six true crime books he had written, he didn't have much free time.

That all might be about to change. He might have more free time than he knew what to do with.

His shoulder throbbed again and he adjusted the sling, gazing out at the stars that had begun to sparkle above the lake.

After hitting rock bottom professionally, with his entire future at the FBI in doubt, where else would he come but home?

He sighed and turned to go back inside. As he did, he spotted the lights still gleaming at the cottage next door, with its blue trim and the porch swing overlooking the water.

She wasn't there now.

Megan Hamilton. Auburn hair, green eyes, a smile that always seemed soft and genuine to everyone else but him.

He drew in a breath, aware of a sharp little twinge of hunger deep in his gut.

When he booked the cottage, he hadn't really thought things through. He should have remembered that Megan and the Inn at Haven Point were a package deal. She owned the inn along with these picturesque little guest cottages on Silver Beach.

He had no idea she actually *lived* in one herself, though. If he had ever heard that little fact, he had forgotten it. Should he have remembered, he would have looked a little harder for a short-term rental property, rather than picking the most convenient lakeshore unit he had found.

Usually, Elliot did his best to avoid her. He wasn't sure why but Megan always left him…unsettled. It had been that way for ages, since long before he learned she and his younger brother had started dating.

He could still remember his shock when he came home for some event or other and saw her and Wyatt together. As in, together, together. Holding hands, sneaking the occasional kiss, giving each other secret smiles. Elliot had felt as if Wyatt had peppered him with buckshot.

He had tried to be happy for his younger brother, one of the most generous, helpful, loving people he'd ever known. Wyatt had been a genuinely good person and deserved to be happy with someone special.

Elliot had felt small and selfish for wishing that someone hadn't been Megan Hamilton.

Watching their glowing happiness together had been tough. He had stayed away for the four or five months they had been dating, though he tried to convince himself it hadn't been on purpose. Work had been demanding and he had been busy carving out his place in the Bureau. He had also started the research that would become his first book, looking into a long-forgotten Montana case from a century earlier where a man had wooed, then married, then killed three spinster schoolteachers from back East for their life insurance money before finally being apprehended by a savvy local sheriff and the sister of one of the dead women.

The few times Elliot returned home during the time Megan had been dating his brother, he had been forced to endure family gatherings knowing she would be there, upsetting his equilibrium and stealing any peace he usually found here.

He couldn't let her do it to him this time.

Her porch light switched off a moment later and Elliot finally breathed a sigh of relief.

He would only be here three weeks. Twenty-one days. Despite the proximity of his cabin to hers, he likely wouldn't even see her much, other than at Katrina's reception.

She would be busy with the inn, with her photography, with her wide circle of friends, while he should be focused on finishing his manuscript and allowing his shoulder to heal—not to mention figuring out whether he would still have a career at the end of that time.

Don't miss THE COTTAGES ON SILVER BEACH
by RaeAnne Thayne,
available July 2018
wherever HQN books and ebooks are sold!

Copyright © 2018 by RaeAnne Thayne

COMING NEXT MONTH FROM

H HARLEQUIN®

SPECIAL EDITION

Available July 17, 2018

#2635 THE MAVERICK'S BABY-IN-WAITING
Montana Mavericks: The Lonelyhearts Ranch • by Melissa Senate
After dumping her cheating fiancé, mom-to-be Mikayla Brown is trying to start fresh—without a man!—but Jensen Jones is determined to pursue her. He's not ready to be a daddy...or is he?

#2636 ADDING UP TO FAMILY
Matchmaking Mamas • by Marie Ferrarella
When widowed rocket scientist Steve Holder needs a housekeeper who can help with his precocious ten-year old, The Matchmaking Mamas know just who to call! But Becky Reynolds soon finds herself in over her head—and on the path to gaining a family!

#2637 SHOW ME A HERO
American Heroes • by Allison Leigh
When small-town cop Ali Templeton shows up at Grant Cooper's door with a baby she says is his niece, the air force vet turned thriller writer is surprised by more than the baby—there's an undeniable attraction to deal with, too. Can he be a hero for more than just the baby's sake? Or will Ali be left out in the cold once again?

#2638 THE BACHELOR'S BABY SURPRISE
Wilde Hearts • by Teri Wilson
After a bad breakup and a one-night stand, Evangeline Holly just wants to forget the whole thing. But it turns out Ryan Wilde is NYC's hottest bachelor, her new boss—and the father of her child!

#2639 HER LOST AND FOUND BABY
The Daycare Chronicles • by Tara Taylor Quinn
Tabitha Jones has teamed up with her food-truck-running neighbor, Johnny Brubaker, to travel to different cities to find her missing son. But as they get closer to bringing Jackson back, they have to decide if they really want their time together to come to an end...

#2640 HIGH COUNTRY COWGIRL
The Brands of Montana • by Joanna Sims
Bonita Delafuente has deferred her dreams to care for her mother. Is falling for Gabe Brand going to force her to choose between love and medical school? Or will her medical history make the choice for her?

YOU CAN FIND MORE INFORMATION ON UPCOMING HARLEQUIN® TITLES, FREE EXCERPTS AND MORE AT WWW.HARLEQUIN.COM.

HSECNM0718

SPECIAL EXCERPT FROM

HARLEQUIN®

SPECIAL EDITION

*When small-town cop Ali Templeton finds the uncle
of an abandoned infant, she wasn't expecting a
famous author—or an undeniable attraction!*

*Read on for a sneak preview of
the next book in the AMERICAN HEROES miniseries,
SHOW ME A HERO,
by* New York Times *bestselling author Allison Leigh.*

"Are you going to ask when you can meet your niece?"

Grant grimaced. "You don't know that she's my niece.
You only think she is."

"It's a pretty good hunch," Ali continued. "If you're
willing to provide a DNA sample, we could know for
sure."

His DNA wouldn't prove squat, though he had no
intention of telling her that. Particularly now that they'd
become the focus of everyone inside the bar. The town
had a whopping population of 5,000. Maybe. It was
small, but that didn't mean there wasn't a chance he'd be
recognized. And the last thing he wanted was a rabid fan
showing up on his doorstep.

He'd had too much of that already. It was one of the
reasons he'd taken refuge at the ranch that his biological
grandparents had once owned. He'd picked it up for a
song when it was auctioned off years ago, but he hadn't
seriously entertained doing much of anything with it—
especially living there himself.

At the time, he'd just taken perverse pleasure in being able to buy up the place where he'd never been welcomed while they'd been alive.

Now it was in such bad disrepair that to stay there even temporarily, he'd been forced to make it habitable.

He wondered if Karen had stayed there, unbeknownst to him. If she was responsible for any of the graffiti or the holes in the walls.

He pushed away the thought and focused on the officer. "Ali. What's it short for?"

She hesitated, obviously caught off guard. "Alicia, but nobody ever calls me that." He'd been edging closer to the door, but she'd edged right along with him. "So, about that—"

Her first name hadn't been on the business card she'd left for him. "Ali fits you better than Alicia."

She gave him a look from beneath her just-from-bed sexy bangs. "Stop changing the subject, Mr. Cooper."

"Start talking about something else, then. Better yet—" he gestured toward the bar and Marty "—start doing the job you've gotta be getting paid for since I can't imagine you slinging drinks just for the hell of it."

Her eyes narrowed and her lips thinned. "Mr. Cooper—"

"G'night, Officer Ali." He pushed open the door and headed out into the night.

Don't miss
SHOW ME A HERO by Allison Leigh,
available August 2018 wherever
Harlequin® Special Edition books and ebooks are sold.

www.Harlequin.com

Copyright © 2018 by Allison Lee Johnson

HSEEXP0718